This book is a work of fiction. The names, characters, places, and incidents are products of the writer's imagination or have been used fictitiously and are not to be construed as real. Any resemblance to persons, living or dead, actual events, locale or organizations is entirely coincidental.

What's worse than learning you have a new sidekick? Finding out it's a know-it-all woman — and she's banging-hot.

When cattle turn up missing, Wyoming lawman Aiden Roshannon is on the scene. There's a reason Aiden's the best at what he does—he only goes by the book. Sure, it's taking some time to track down the criminals who are stealing and outright butchering the good ranchers' animals, but he'll serve them justice in the end.

Amaryllis Long has been a Texas Ranger for five years and her experience trumps anything this newbie operation in Wyoming has seen. She's locked and loaded, ready to break all the rules if it means getting her criminal cuffed and stuffed. Only thing is, she needs an extra set of cuffs for her sidekick Aiden. The lawman might be hunky as hell with hidden tattoos and secrets as long as a summer's day, but she knows best.

Asking Amaryllis to stop and think before she acts is like asking a pig to stop eating. She's reckless, annoying… and a damn good kisser. Half the time Aiden doesn't know if he wants to throw her in the back of the truck and have his way with her or hog-tie her and leave her alongside the road. They might both be fighting for the same goal but if they can't agree on how to handle the situation, how can they succeed?

Something About a Lawman

by

Em Petrova

Chapter One

Aiden Roshannon had been to some bonfires in his day. As a kid on the ranch, it was a ritual at the end of each harvest for his pa to throw a huge bash for all the hired hands and neighbors. In his teens, there was always a party involving a wall of fire some idiot had hosed down with gasoline while they all drank beers and pretended they were grown up.

But this particular bonfire he wished he could sneak away from. One of the sheriff's deputies had invited him. Bullied him, if he was honest. It wasn't that Aiden didn't like the deputy — he just didn't like his friends.

Hoyt stood off to the side, holding a beer, joking to one of his buddies from up north of Crossroads. Wyoming was a big state, but it seemed nobody had a problem with drinking too much and then driving too far to get home.

Aiden sat in a lawn chair facing the fire, his cowboy boot crossed over his knee and his beer growing warm in his grip. The loud bark of laughter from Hoyt's friend made him grit his teeth. Aiden had met Cody Shivis before. He thought him a dickhead then and he thought him a dickhead now.

Several ladies came out of the darkness into the ring of firelight, giggling after their trip to the bathroom. A blonde was tipsy enough without the uneven ground, and she nearly pitched headfirst into the flames.

Aiden shot out of his seat and caught her. "Whoa, there. Let's get you a chair."

Holding onto her waist, he guided her to his lawn chair. She settled too hard and the chair tipped back on its legs. With quick instincts, Aiden planted his palms on her thighs and settled the legs on the ground again.

"What the fuck're you doing touching my woman?"

Aiden recognized that obnoxious voice and turned just as a fist missiled at his eye. He couldn't have dodged if he'd wanted — it was too late. Knuckles connected with eye socket. Stars exploded in his vision and he stumbled back a step, conscious he didn't want to land in the fire either.

He used his jaw to draw his face down so his eye opened. Shivis swung at him again, but this time Aiden was ready.

Women screamed. The fire crackled, logs shifted, sparks flew up to the sky, dotting it orange against the midnight black.

Anger tore through Aiden as the pain in his eye meshed with the spurt of adrenaline racing through his veins.

"What the fuck's the matter with you? I was just keepin' your woman from falling into the fire. She's sopping drunk and you should take her home. Oh wait, you're soused too."

"You touched my girl. Nobody touches my girl." Shivis's face was livid, a mask contorting in the strange flicker of firelight.

Aiden moved in a half-circle in front of the row of lawn chairs and log stools drawn close to the fire ring. There wasn't enough room to fight here without somebody else getting hurt.

"Let's take this on over there. In the yard."

"Fight! Fight!" someone screamed.

Shivis gave a hard nod and walked away, a cocky sway in his drunken walk. If Aiden fought dirty, he'd jump the guy from behind, but he didn't roll that way.

He followed with several people on his tail, rabid for the pending fight.

In the center of the yard, Shivis threw his arms up to the sky. It was darker over here, the firelight no help, and only a dim garage light giving Aiden an outline of his opponent's body.

"Now, Roshannon, you don't need to fight him. I'll give him another beer and he'll pass out and won't remember a thing in the morning." Hoyt was his angel of good on one shoulder.

Then there was the other shoulder. The one with the devil, urging Aiden to whoop this guy's ass once and for all.

"Yeah, but I'll remember." He stepped toward his opponent. The crowd of about twenty people gathered around them. Hemmed them in, more like. Aiden glared at the man before him and gauged his reaction times. Three beers an hour for the past three hours had to put his blood alcohol level up around .20.

Severe motor discoordination and lack of judgment. But the guy was drunk enough not to feel pain and that meant he'd keep coming no matter how many punches Aiden threw.

He just had to knock him out with the first blow.

Shivis was a class-A douche bag and he treated that woman he was championing like dirt, stepping out on her every chance he got. Judging by the ladies he chose, he had to be bringing home a new STD weekly.

Hoyt threw out an arm in front of Aiden. He turned his glare from Shivis to his own work colleague. A year in the sheriff's office together meant they were friends. But all that could be ruined tonight.

4

"I don't know why you hang out with this stupid ass, Hoyt. You're smart."

Hoyt pressed his lips together. "He's a buddy from high school."

"High school was a long time ago. Time to get a new set of friends." He pushed by Hoyt and stepped up to Shivis.

The man swayed back and forth as if fighting for equilibrium. Hell, this would be easy. Aiden felt the knot between his shoulders relax as he raised his fists. "I'll give you the first punch, man. After that, I'm no gentleman."

Shivis's teeth gleamed white as he cocked his fist and threw it with everything he had toward Aiden's nose. Aiden dodged his head to the side almost lazily. Laughter rippled from behind him, as well as a few "oh no's."

Aiden grinned back and then delivered a right hook to Shivis's jaw that rocked his head. He nearly fell over but somehow remained upright, head lowered and spittle and blood dripping from his jaw.

"You no-good Marine traitor. Leavin' your men and our country when you tucked tail and ran."

Aiden let the insult roll off him. It wasn't anything he hadn't heard before. But it wasn't true either. He loved his country and his men were never in jeopardy.

"That's all you got, Shivis? Nothing better you can think of?" Aiden drawled. His eye hurt like a motherfucker and he knew the bruise was already collecting around it.

"You're a woman beater too. Got whips and shit, I hear."

"You been in my bedroom and find them?" Aiden's response drew laughter.

"You're a sick fucker and a traitor and now you're working for the sheriff, when you should be shoveling shit."

"Shovelin' shit's an honest living."

Many nods answered him from the shadows.

"Give it to him good, Roshannon! Asshole needs to shut up," someone called.

The corner of Aiden's mouth turned up. He clenched his fist and jabbed Shivis in the stomach, then caught him with an uppercut to the jaw that sent him backward onto the ground, flat out.

"Oh my God, you killed him!" The blonde who was his girlfriend ran to Shivis and dropped to her knees. "He's dead. He pissed himself!"

Aiden walked up and looked down to see the guy's chest moving. "He's not dead. He's knocked out. Someone get him a blanket and let him sleep it off." He flexed his fingers and headed toward the driveway and his truck.

"Thanks for invitin' me, Hoyt. Haven't had this much fun in ages. Now I've got to get home to polish my whips and Marine Corps lapel pin." He strutted off without a backward glance.

* * * * *

"Roshannon."

Aiden looked up at his last name to see Hoyt in the doorway of his office, his big bulk blocking everything behind him. He stared at him steadily. "Everything okay at your place after last night?"

Hoyt winced. "Nice eye. Put a steak on it?"

"Yeah." He fingered the edges of the black bruise. "Didn't do much good. By the time I got home, it was already bruised."

"I'm sorry about Shivis. He *is* an asshole. Especially when he's drunk."

"No hard feelings. You can be friends with whoever you want." *I just won't be coming to any more of your parties.*

The sound of voices projected from behind Hoyt. Aiden craned to look around him. "Did you need something?"

"Oh yeah. Some people here to talk to ya."

7

He rounded the desk and Hoyt moved aside to let him see a group of men congregated in the office. Cattle ranchers, each as hardened by hard work and determination as the next. Boots, hats and Carhartts were the general attire.

"This problem is growing—the crime is out of control. What are you gonna do about it?" one demanded, his eyes flashing at the sheriff.

Aiden pushed out of his office, which was more of a cubicle crammed in the corner of the sheriff's office building, the bigger spaces for the deputies. He'd found a lot of people didn't want to hire an ex-military man with a questionable past, but he'd found a home here as a special investigator.

Thank God, because the last thing he'd wanted was to take up his twin brother—and sheriff of the next county—on his offer of a position under him.

"Where's Roshannon? Ain't he in charge of finding out who took our cattle?" the rancher asked.

Aiden pushed his way to the front of the group and looked at the posse of angry men. He glanced to the sheriff. "Fill me in."

Sheriff Latchaw pushed his fingers through his gray hair.

"Five cattle missing from Dan's place here."

"And two from mine."

"Last week I had some hay stolen."

"I've been looking into that, Niles." Aiden looked the man in the eyes. Not many leads, and it was frustrating as hell for both parties.

"What are ya doing about all this thieving going on, Roshannon? Sheriff?" Dan tugged his battered ridge-top hat lower and glared.

"Hoyt here will be happy to take your statement. Roshannon and I will be with you after that," Latchaw said.

Aiden nodded. He had no idea what the sheriff had up his sleeve, but he steeled himself. He'd had too many commanding officers to think Latchaw would speak to him privately about anything good.

Hoyt led Dan and a few others off to take their statements, and Aiden followed Latchaw into his office.

"Close the door."

Here it was. Aiden didn't know if he could keep his damn mouth shut for the sheriff the way he had his CO or any of his other superiors when they'd interrogated him for hours on end, day after day until they got the answers that would finally satisfy them enough to give him an honorable discharge.

Latchaw leaned against his desk and folded his arms. "We've got a mess on our hands here with these thefts. It's more than a few and we don't want the cattle association losing faith in our abilities to do our jobs."

"I agree." Aiden bit off the urge to end that sentence with an automatic *sir*. "I'm headed to auction later this afternoon, up in Riverton."

He nodded. "Good. That's a start. Looking for the cattle brands at the auction is the quickest route to finding who is thievin'. But I've been thinking on this problem a while now. Theft is up across the state, and many of the sheriffs are in the same boat as we are. Angry ranchers demanding information on the crimes."

"So what are the others saying?" Aiden felt his emotions switch off, just as he had after the *incident*. The one that had caused so much fury and humiliation on his part, the one Shivis had brought up the previous night.

Nobody knew what had happened—it was classified. If they knew he'd refused to open fire on a building filled with innocent lives even if there *was* an ISIS group operating out of it too, maybe they wouldn't throw stones. All the general population knew was he was investigated. The rest was speculation.

"They're saying we need more than a few men scattered around investigating these crimes. We've got Michaelson five counties over and Bridges down south. It's not enough, not with the number of reports we have coming in right now of cattle being stolen."

"I've been putting in overtime. Talked to three ranchers yesterday."

"I know you're doing what you can. But it's time to make a change. Add more feet to the ground. We need to band together."

"Like the Texas Rangers?" Aiden's pulse throbbed in his temples. He was getting one of his stress migraines.

Latchaw nodded. "Exactly like that. Congratulations, Special Investigator Roshannon. You're heading it. You have leave to operate in all counties of Wyoming."

Aiden blinked. "This wasn't what I was expecting."

"You're one of the most precise, organized lawmen I've ever met. That book of yours is testament to that." He nodded toward Aiden's shirt, where he kept the small journal of notes on each case.

Aiden resisted the urge to touch his breast pocket. "I appreciate that, sir."

"Well-deserved. I know you're the best man for the job."

Excitement was taking hold—a foreign fluttery feeling he hadn't experienced in many years. Not much riled him up these days. Hell, the mention of his whips the previous night had been the only lift of mood he'd felt in too long.

"It's a big job, though." Latchaw eyed him.

"I'll do a good one."

"You will, but there's a lot of work to be done and territory to cover. Which is why I'm pulling in a consultant. Someone who's covered a huge amount of ground over the years and brought in a lot of rustlers."

Aiden stared at the sheriff. He didn't like that smirk on his face, not one bit. "Who is it? Do I know him?"

Just what he needed—an annoying know-it-all telling him how to conduct investigations.

Latchaw's smirk stretched into a smile. "You don't know *him*. But you might know this name—Amaryllis Long."

Oh shit.

"The Texas Ranger woman?"

"That's right. Ms. Long will be calling in to speak with you and go over a few cases before the day's end. Then maybe you can... I don't know, what do they call it? Skype or something. Keep in touch with what's happening." Latchaw circled his desk and plopped into the leather chair that had probably held him up for two decades. It molded to his form like a comfy armchair. "Good luck, lawman."

Aiden muttered a thanks and tugged the brim of his hat on the way out the door. His mind was spinning at the mere mention of a name. Amaryllis Long. She was known for being a huge pain in the ass to sheriffs and police all over Texas. Now she was going to be his personal pain-in-the-ass.

He went into his office and pulled out his journal. In neat letters, he wrote the date and time. Then he added the details of today's crimes, including the names of the ranchers and their claims. He'd get more details from Hoyt later.

At the bottom of the page, he added one more note, scribbled instead of written neatly.

A name.

Amaryllis Long.

Chapter Two

"Long, this is Marlena. Over."

The call came in over the CB radio in Amaryllis's truck. Her only communication with the people she worked with and the other lawmen of Texas. Marlena kept her up to date on the new calls coming in about cattle thefts, and she was a sweetheart of a woman.

She plucked up the CB unit from its hook on her dashboard and pressed the button. "Go ahead, Marlena."

"I've got Special Investigator Roshannon calling you in five minutes to go over his cases."

"Oh damn, is that today?"

"Yes." Marlena's tone tinged with amusement.

"Okay. I'm headed south to speak to the state representative. He wants that statement from me. Publicity stunt, pure and simple. He wants people to believe he supports agriculture and the ranchers should all vote for him."

"Most likely. Plus, you're a pretty face for a photo shoot, Amaryllis."

Amaryllis grunted. The last thing she wanted was to be considered for her pretty face. Being known as a kick-ass Texas Ranger was all she expected. Who gave a damn what she looked like as long as she was bringing in the criminals?

"Thanks for reminding me about Roshannon."

Her cell rang. "There he is now. Talk to you later, Marlena. You can tell me all about those naughty kids of yours and what pranks they've pulled this week."

"Oh, I've got a doozy of a tale for you. Speak soon, Amaryllis."

She hooked the CB back in its holder and grabbed her cell. "Amaryllis Long."

A beat of silence.

"Hello?"

"Hello. This is Roshannon, Aiden Roshannon from Crossroads."

His deep voice projecting through her truck speakers made her feel the man was sitting in the truck with her. While she'd had plenty of other Rangers working with her, she'd never directly noticed a voice the way she did Roshannon's.

"I hear you've got a heap of trouble up your way," she said.

"That's right. Something big going on here, too many cattle thefts to be random."

"Probably a group working together. Splitting profits."

"That's running through my mind too."

Good—they were on the same page.

"There's also some butcherings going on."

"Ah. I've seen that a time or ten as well. Fill me in." She listened for five minutes as Roshannon recited all the events and details. He sounded as though he was reading from a book.

She cut across him. "Where are you seeing most activity?"

When he responded, irritation sounded in his voice. "It's scattered. Look, I'm not sure why I'm telling you these things. You don't have any idea what's going on in Wyoming."

She almost rolled her eyes, but she'd gotten good at stopping that habit. Men didn't like women rolling their eyes at them and then one-upping them on the job. Even though Roshannon couldn't see her.

"Look, I've got five years under my belt. I've seen plenty and rustlers are rustlers, no matter what part of the country."

"I'm pretty sure I'm taking all the measures you do. This call is just a formality."

Because his boss had asked Roshannon to consult with her.

"I see. Well, you do what you need to do up there in Wyoming, Roshannon. You know where to find me if you need any advice."

She kept her tone cool and even, though she wanted to scream and hurl things at her cell phone. The man wasn't any different from most of those she came in contact with. Ranchers who called her *sweet thing* and dismissed her to speak with another man who knew much less.

"Thanks for your time," Roshannon said.

"Goodbye." She ended the call and stared at the road ahead of her, seething. By this time in her career, she should be used to being treated like an imbecile. Why should a female know a thing about cattle? Land sakes, she should be in the kitchen making biscuits. In her line of business, the year may as well be 1950, while she operated in present day. An age where a woman was a Texas Ranger and did a fine fucking job at it too.

She breathed a heavy sigh through her nostrils and tried to shake off Roshannon's call. He didn't think she was worth his time. Well, good luck to him. She'd seen big operations like he was describing before, and it wasn't something a man could take down on his own. The way Sheriff Latchaw had made it sound,

17

there weren't many investigating cattle crimes in Wyoming and they needed all the help they could get.

Stubborn ass of a man.

Every time she met someone, expecting to be treated as an equal, she came away angry and disappointed in humanity. By now, she should have known Roshannon would be no different.

She continued on down the highway.

He did have a yummy voice, though.

Later, when she stopped, she'd Google him and see what she could dig up on the man. He was probably an ugly cuss, with a face only a mother could love.

Within half an hour, she'd reached her destination. As she walked toward the office of the state representative, she steeled herself. Being used for votes didn't sit well with her, and she'd give this guy a piece of her mind, same as she had Roshannon.

Amaryllis wasn't a woman to roll over and take commands.

* * * * *

When Aiden's twin answered his cell on the fourth ring, Aiden said, "Dude, you're pretty fucking hard to track down."

"Hello to you too, Mr. Merry Sunshine. What's crawled up your ass already this morning? It's only eight-thirty."

"Been trying to call you for hours."

"Got the messages. Didn't have time to answer them. We've got big trouble up here, a cold case reopened suddenly when we got word this guy's been bragging about killing a woman."

"Does it seem to be true?"

"I'd like to hazard a guess and say yeah, since he saw us coming and ran for it. Spent all night hunting his ass all over the county. Then he crossed the border and I had to work with that county's sheriff's department, but it seems we lost him. For now. He has a warrant out, so now the suspect's gotta answer to Wes."

"Must be a big case if you've already sicced our bounty hunter cousin on him."

"Benefit of havin' law in the family." There was a smile in Judd's voice.

"Exactly my thinking, which is why I was calling."

"More trouble your way with the rustlers?"

"Yeah, and people are starting to freak out. I've caught a few guys stealing, but there is definitely a bigger operation going on here. Overnight, five gone from Owens' pasture.

19

And another found dead, butchered on the road."

"Jesus, are you serious? I can only imagine what that must have looked like, the blood on the road and a carcass left behind."

"Scared the nipples off a woman coming home late from the night shift. I've been up all night." He rubbed at his unshaven jaw and it rasped beneath his knuckles.

Judd grunted. "Poor woman. So, you need help with the case?"

"Not exactly, but I'm getting help anyway." Aiden stared at the overflowing garbage can in his office. Around two a.m., he'd decided his desk was overrun with papers and purged it. All the while, his brain had been working overtime on the case and he'd kept stopping to scribble notes to himself.

And think about the woman who he'd spoken with several times. Amaryllis Long wasn't as pleasant as her voice suggested. Each time she copped that know-it-all tone, he wanted to wring her neck. After five phone calls, each forced by Sheriff Latchaw, he was about to go against orders again and refuse to speak with Amaryllis. Even though one of her suggestions about evidence had panned out, she didn't have to sound so smug about it.

"What are you talkin' about, Aiden? I don't exactly have spare time for chitchat."

"Neither do I. What do you know about Amaryllis Long?"

Silence on the other end. Aiden could almost see Judd gnawing his lower lip as he was prone to do. Then his brother let out a long breath. "Heard she's the best at catching rustlers down in Texas."

"I'm working with her on these cases. Against my will."

"Against your will? Latchaw set you up with her."

"That's right. And she is as irritating as they come. Easier to talk to a damn rooster."

As kids, they'd had a rooster named Mr. Banty who never shut up from dawn till dusk. Finally, their pa had shot him for their dinner because he was so irritating.

"If Latchaw set you up, he has good reason. He's seen his fair share of similar operations, and this must be big if he's bringing in consultants," Judd said.

"So you know of her."

"Yeah, I do. She's coming here to help you with the case?"

God, he hoped not. Talking to her on the phone was bad enough. Even though between her snotty words, he liked the sound of her voice. All husky, raspy even. Like she'd screamed all night in pleasure.

21

"I don't think she's coming to Wyoming. Latchaw foisted her onto me, and I don't feel like she's helping much. It's just another thing on my to-do list, you know?"

Judd was quiet a minute.

"Shit. What do you know?" Aiden demanded.

"I knew all about you speaking with Amaryllis."

"Why didn't you just come out and says so?"

"I wanted to hear what you said first."

"What else do you know? I hear in your tone that you're withholding information, Judd." Aiden pulled off his hat and glared at nothing and everything. Right now, he was ready to spit nails. He hated when Judd held info over him.

"Aren't you supposed to Skype with the woman?"

Fuck. Triple fuck with biscuits and gravy.

"Who told you that? Latchaw?"

Judd issued a low whistle. "You don't have any idea what you're in for, brother."

"What do you mean? She's pretty?"

"Don't you ever use the Internet, Aiden? You act like you were born in another century. Open up a browser and type in her name."

"I'll do it later. I'm away from my desk."
He wasn't. He just wasn't about to do it while
Judd was on the line.

"Look her up. Not only is she beautiful,
but she's intense."

"Intense how? She's a nagging woman, I
know that much." She'd been riding him with
questions every time they were on the phone.
Now she'd do it face-to-face on a damn Skype
call.

"I mean she's protective of her cattle
ranchers like a momma bison is to her young."

"We all feel that way. That's nothing to
note."

"I mean like I'll-throw-a-pipe-bomb-
through-your-windows-motherfucker kind of
protect. She goes all out to apprehend her
suspects, even if it means going in the back
door of the law. You're working with the best,
Aiden. My advice is take advantage of it. And
enjoy your Skype call. I heard you've got a
doozy of a black eye to show her."

"Fuck off." Aiden rubbed a hand over his
face. Great—all he needed was a woman who
wouldn't follow the rules. Aiden couldn't be
associated with someone who wouldn't—he'd
gotten himself in plenty of trouble in the
military for exactly the same thing.

"Shit," he said quietly.

"Just think of what you'll learn from having new eyes on the case. Remember that time we let Sadie Townsend into our detective club?"

He groaned. "Don't remind me. Disaster."

"At least you got to kiss her."

"But she was flirting with you and Wes the whole time she was there."

"We all had crushes on her."

"That's when we learned family sticks together and girls can't interfere with that."

"Right. But I'll call you tonight and see how it went with Amaryllis. I know you've got a thing for brown-eyed girls."

Fuck. He didn't want the image of Amaryllis in his head right now. He was tired and if she was as beautiful as his brother said, he'd just end up being horny, staring at the dust on his paddle and flogger.

Judd said something to another person on his end. Then he said, "Aiden, I gotta run. Sighting of a man running through somebody's back yard. Might be our man. Good luck."

"You too."

Aiden hung up and stared at the trash again. Maybe he'd better tidy up before he Skyped Amaryllis. Not that she'd see more than his face on the screen.

Judd's words filtered into his brain again. *Like I'll-throw-a-pipe-bomb-through-your-windows-motherfucker kind of protect.*

Great. He was dealing with someone who was as crazy as him.

A rap on the door made him look up to see Latchaw standing there, looking every bit the old-school sheriff. Big white hat, face lined but animated. "Need ya in my office, Roshannon."

Aiden stood and followed, knowing what was to come. He wasn't afraid of a little video chat, but he didn't know how to keep the annoyed looks off his face. When he spoke to Amaryllis on the phone, she couldn't see him shaking his head or pinching the bridge of his nose in frustration.

He went into Latchaw's office.

"Close the door."

He did, feeling one of his stress migraines squeezing at his temples again. All of a sudden, he was back in the interrogation room, being asked where his loyalties lay and thwarting rumors that he was a terrorist.

He dragged in a deep breath. He wasn't in the Marines anymore, and Latchaw wasn't investigating him.

"I've got Amaryllis on standby here." Latchaw pressed a button on his keyboard and a face popped onto his screen.

25

Aiden's breath whooshed from him. He stared at the woman he'd been talking to, wishing like hell he'd gotten a chance to Google her like Judd had suggested.

Nothing could have prepared him for seeing those big, brown melted-chocolate eyes on screen. Or the strawberry blonde hair. Her coloring was pale, pointing toward her hair color being real and not a dye job. But those dark eyes made him question it.

Delicate bones, a wide forehead tapering down to high cheekbones and a pointed chin. Her lips full, the lower lip fuller. Kissable. Bitable.

His groin took a hit at that thought. Too long since he'd had a submissive on her knees for him. He really needed to listen to his brother and cousin and get out in the dating field again.

Finding a woman who suited his tastes was another problem, though. Shivis hadn't been completely off-base in suggesting Aiden had darker inclinations in the bedroom.

"Amaryllis, this is Roshannon."

She stared out of the screen at him. Her eyes deep enough to fall into. She sat back in her chair, giving him a new view of her. Revealing a slender neck and a plaid shirt that he'd bet his sidearm was straining across the breasts.

His cock stirred behind his fly.

He tugged his hat brim to cover his discomposure. Judd hadn't warned him—not even close. Amaryllis wasn't just beautiful—she was drop-dead gorgeous. Banging-hot. The things he could do with those plump lips...

"Take a seat, Roshannon. I filled in Amaryllis about yesterday's events. She has some suggestions of where to start our search."

Aiden took a seat and tried for a casual expression. He was failing miserably, he knew by the little image of himself in the lower corner of the screen. He looked tense, ready for battle.

He relaxed his grip on the armrests and nodded to Amaryllis. "Uh—What are your thoughts?"

"You're looking in far too obvious places. You're looking at a list of people who've committed crimes in your counties or the surrounding counties."

Aiden shot a glance at Latchaw, who was nodding. "That's right."

"I had a case where several Rangers believed our suspect was a guy with five counts of felonies already and had served seven years on a prior. But I couldn't see it. I believe you're dealing with something similar—it's not obvious."

"So what do you suggest?" he said tightly. So roughly that Latchaw threw him a look.

Amaryllis shifted in her chair, bringing those bouncy breasts upward as she settled in a new position. Aiden's jeans got pretty damn tight, and he had to control his breathing. The things she was doing to his body… He could almost feel the handle of his paddle in his palm.

He closed his fist and thumped it in a light rhythm on the armrest. Distraction. He couldn't be looking at this woman in such a way. She drove him crazy — and not in a sexual way.

She was talking and he missed what she said. Dammit.

She tipped her head in an adorable way, a way that called out to him with all the sass he loved in a submissive. Oh, she could be tamed. The little wildcat just didn't know it yet.

Yet? Roshannon, you can't do a damn thing with this woman. She's off-limits, she's like seven states away. And she's a pain in the ass.

She'd have a pain in her backside if he ever got near her. He knew exactly how he'd get her in hand.

Fuck.

"You're not paying attention to anything I'm saying, are you, Roshannon? You think

28

you're the first guy to ever ignore my suggestions?" She sat back and folded her arms, which only pushed her breasts out more.

He groaned inwardly. This was bad on so many levels. Not only were her tits the most mouth-watering delights he'd seen in his life, but the sheriff—his boss—stood a few feet away listening to her tell off Aiden for thinking she was worthless in this position.

There were sooooo many other positions for her.

Double fuck.

He pushed out a breath and attempted to grab hold of the reins. "Look, Amaryllis. I believe you know your stuff. Your track record is testimony to that."

She only tipped her head in that "what else?" way. Cute, charming and fucking annoying at the same time.

"I just don't believe you can tell us what to look for when you're in Texas. You don't know the area. The terrain is even a factor. For instance, a rancher settled between mountains with one road in to his property and a locked gate on it to keep out trespassers has five cows missing. There's not a lot of ways in to his property to steal them. The mountains run right up to his borders. You can't see what we're dealing with."

God help him, she drew her lower lip between her teeth and worried it for a split second. But it was enough to set his teeth on edge, his cock at full attention.

He fisted his hand so hard his knuckle popped.

Latchaw stepped toward the desk and toward the screen with Amaryllis staring out of it. "Seems like there's only one way for you to see—come to Wyoming. I'll have a ticket booked for you within the hour. Keep an eye out for the email confirmation."

Amaryllis blinked and then nodded. "Thank you. I'm honored to be invited." She directed her gaze at Aiden. "Roshannon. Guess I'll be seeing you soon. You can tell me all about that black eye then."

Chapter Three

Amaryllis flipped open a newspaper she'd snagged in the airport. The man beside her in first-class shot her a dirty look for making noise, so she rattled the pages again and met his gaze.

She'd been told she had a glare that could make a grown man's balls shrivel, but she wouldn't claim that title yet. She was sure to meet a few more in her lifetime who would make her earn it.

Working with hard-ass ranchers and lawmen wasn't easy, and she always had her mental boxing gloves at the ready. Two older brothers and a protective father had taught her all she needed to know about dealing with assholes. She'd managed to run them around in circles by the time she was out of pigtails. When she wasn't conjuring snappy comebacks to her big brothers' insults, she was learning all she could about dealing with men on her daddy's ranch.

Men who said she couldn't do this or that, shouldn't try. She'd shown them all and then some.

She crossed her legs and her paper rustled again. She ignored the fresh glare from her neighbor and stared at a headline for a cattle theft. A small headline, barely noticeable amid stories of the small-town pie-eating contest and a list of bike nights in the Wyoming county.

Bovine Bandits Strike Again.

Honestly, who wrote these things? Amusement tipped the corner of her lips as she read. She skipped the cutesy puns about beef burglars and focused on the particulars. Time, place, what the cattle were worth. Any leads. And of course, the investigator on the scene.

Why, land sakes. They even got a quote from the man. Aiden Roshannon, the man of few words. "Cattle theft is no light matter, and I am committed to tracking down the perpetrators. When someone comes onto your land and steals something that means a lot to you, something that means your livelihood, well, that means war around these parts."

She lowered the paper a bit and looked toward the small jet window that revealed a glimmer of sun in an otherwise cloudy sky. Her first impression of Roshannon wasn't great. But his dedication to the job was something she could respect. Maybe after they cut the bullshit between them and she set her ground rules for how he'd treat her, he wouldn't be such a dweeb to work with, after all.

She couldn't deny she was excited for some new turf. New ranchers to meet, new challenges to accept. But then there was Roshannon. Working conditions could be hell, despite how attractive he was.

Outright hot if she was honest. Dark hair, a fine, straight nose. Piercing eyes that unnerved her, and it wasn't just the black bruise he sported that gave her pause. Something about the way he eyed her made her feel hot and sweaty.

She'd done a little research on the guy. He had no social media to speak off and found only a headline for a small-town newspaper announcing hometown pride for him joining the Marines years ago.

There had been a tiny photo of Roshannon, smiling, looking like a kid with stars and stripes in his eyes. Going off to serve his country. Now he was protecting and serving cattle ranchers, but she liked the attitude of his quote.

She closed the paper and folded it to stow in her tote bag. Then she pulled out a computer tablet and started flipping through the screens until she reached the file with all her research on it.

A lot of cattle killings in Wyoming. People who slaughtered cows for the meat weren't that uncommon. People did stupid things or were just plain desperate. In Texas, poverty ran high in some parts, and people needed food. Of course, once she caught them and they served jail time for their acts or paid hefty fines, they wished they'd taken a deer or wild hog instead of an expensive beef cow.

Prices were on the rise, almost double for a calf now. And that meant people saw dollar signs. She'd learned quick that money was always a motive, and traveling the auctions around the state and as far out as Kansas usually ended up with a person in handcuffs.

Cattle rustlers weren't just for the Old West. They were alive and well, and the reason Amaryllis had a job.

A job she was passionate about.

She didn't have any wifi on this flight, but she'd gotten a bunch of emails just before she boarded the plane. One was from her bank— info about a mortgage she'd applied for. And one from her brother JD.

JD was only a year older, but he loved to lord it over her. He'd been travelling the South rodeoin', and he was earning enough of a living not to come home the entire past year. Their daddy hadn't been all that happy with JD staying away. The ranch always needed more hands, and Amaryllis was too involved with the Rangers to be much assistance. That left their oldest sibling Ulyss to rule the roost.

And Lord, did he crow about it too. Every time Amaryllis spoke to him, he paused half a dozen times to boss someone around.

JD had emailed some of the information she'd asked him for concerning her dream of running her own place. A small farm had come up for sale about fifty miles from where she'd been raised. One day she'd been driving by it on her way to investigate some stolen cattle when she'd spotted the sign. After backing up, she'd pulled into a dirt drive and found her heart fluttering fast.

The land was beautiful, flat and green, ready for seeds to be sown. But she was a rancher's daughter. She knew about raising beef and hay, not other crops. Not like what she had in mind.

The plane dipped suddenly, and her stomach with it. She lowered the tablet and looked out at the clouds. The ray of sun she'd seen before had vanished, leaving only a dark gray gloom. They were flying into a storm.

Another big bump, and she gripped the arm of the seat. She'd flown enough in her day to be no stranger to turbulence, but that didn't mean she liked it.

She stared at the little window. A streak of lightning had her teeth clamped together. But she didn't look away. Somehow, seeing what was coming was better than guessing.

Another big pocket of rough air and the pilot came on the loudspeaker to tell them he'd be climbing higher to get above the storm.

"This better not make us late getting on the ground," the passenger beside her said. "I have a connecting flight."

Amaryllis didn't respond.

"Well, I guess there's nothing to do but get comfortable." The man kicked off his shoes.

"Seriously? Put your shoes back on," she said.

"Lady, I paid for this seat and all the space I get around it. What I do here is none of your business."

She glared at him and then looked pointedly at his loafers with the stupid little tassels and then back to him. He just closed his eyes and leaned back in his seat.

She breathed shallowly. She hadn't caught a whiff of the weird man's feet, but she wasn't about to breathe deeply and find out if she would. She twisted away toward the window, preferring the storm over an inconsiderate ass.

After they climbed in altitude, it was apparent they were not flying out of this storm.

The plane tilted sharply and a few squeals of surprise sounded from the passengers in coach. She tried to focus on her brother's email attachments about success rates for certain crops and what they went to market for. But after another long patch of turbulence, she gave up.

Her eyes were beginning to throb with a small headache, but she watched the sky the way she'd watch a road. She hated flying mainly because she wanted to be in control.

The man next to her hitched his ankle over his knee, bringing his socked foot inches from her leg.

"You cross this line, buddy, and we're gonna throw down," she bit off.

He opened his eyes and gave her a smile that made her realize he was trying to goad her. Like so many men in her past, brothers included. Well, she knew exactly how to deal with him.

She leaned over and fished around in her tote until she found her flight-sized bottle of hand lotion. She squeezed a small amount into her hand and a generous glop into his shoe.

She sat back with a smile, rubbing her hands together to work in the lotion.

He wrinkled his nose. "Can't you wait to do that? Flowery smells give me migraines."

She smiled her sweetest smile reserved for really big jerks. "I paid for this seat and all the space around it. What I do in it is none of your business."

He grunted and closed his eyes again. She leaned over while he snored and filled up his other shoe with lotion. Then she watched the storm roll in from the North.

* * * * *

Amaryllis needed a drink—now. After the bumpiest descent of her life, ending in what felt like the jet falling out of the sky onto the runway, only alcohol could settle her nerves. Her fingers were cramped from gripping the armrest. But it *had* been amusing when her neighbor put his shoes back on.

Saying he was irate was like saying roosters don't crow. Thankfully, she was one of the first passengers off the plane, leaving his bitching about her being immature and a terrible human being behind.

She practically swayed on her feet. Yep, liquid fortification. Now.

"Where's the nearest bar?" she asked a woman at a desk.

She pointed, and Amaryllis felt a huge surge of relief that it wasn't too many steps away. She clutched the handle of her wheeled carryon and dragged it as fast as she could through the people milling around the airport.

She was in Wyoming, and so far she didn't think much of the damn state. People claimed Texas storms were so big and nasty that God Himself cast them. But Wyoming seemed to be trying to outdo her home state.

Torrents of water struck the building, making it sound hollow despite all the noise of activity. At one point when they were coming in for a landing, she swore there was hail bouncing off the jet.

She straightened her shoulders and dragged her luggage through the entrance of the lounge. The long, polished bar gleamed from rubbing, and glass bottles lined the space behind. She claimed a seat toward the end and ordered tequila at the same time.

The bartender gave her a slight smile as he set the glass before her. "I'll need another," she said before tossing it back her throat neatly.

"Rough flight?"

"You could say that." She wasn't afraid of much, and definitely not storms. But she still felt off-kilter after that trip.

He gave her another shot of tequila, and she sipped this one more slowly. Savoring the burn and the notes of alcohol playing on her tongue. In the background, a rerun TV show played, somehow contributing to her feeling of normal.

A man dropped onto a stool next to her. She gave him the side-eye. Of all the places to sit along the long, empty bar, he chose the seat beside her. She knew this song and dance.

She took another sip of tequila as he ordered a double of Jack.

While the bartender poured his drink, the man looked at her. "Were you on that flight from Texas? That was somethin'." Him being from Texas didn't make them buddies.

She nodded out of politeness.

"Could have used this in the air," he said, wrapping his fingers around his shot glass. He wore two big knuckle rings that were brighter than any sun she'd probably ever see in Wyoming.

He shifted on his stool, never looking away from her. "You from Texas?"

"Right now I'm from this barstool."

He laughed, but she hadn't meant it to be funny. "Well, that amuses me, sweet stuff. I guess I'll make this one my home and we can be neighbors."

Fabulous.

She just wanted to sip her tequila in peace.

"Anyone ever tell you how pretty you are?"

"These lines won't work."

"It's not a line, sweet stuff. You're downright beautiful. Saw you first thing when I walked in the bar."

That was because she was sitting nearest the entrance. He'd have to be blind not to see her.

"All that strawberry blonde hair..."

If he asked if the rug matched the drapes, she was going to bash him over the head with her suitcase.

Luckily, he sipped his whiskey and only eyed her. "What brings you to Wyoming? Maybe we can cross paths while we're here."

She wouldn't be surprised if he actually owned another ring — a wedding band — and he just wasn't wearing it. He was certainly giving her a scum-of-the-earth vibe.

"I'm here on business and I definitely don't want to cross paths with you." She met the bartender's eyes and knocked back the rest of her drink. "I'll pay for the shots now."

She got off the stool and dragged her luggage with her, ignoring the way the man sitting at the bar followed her with his gaze. She was glad she hadn't taken a third shot, because she wanted to get in her rental car and away from here as quickly as possible. She wasn't a prissy girl by any means, but the day's events had exhausted her already and it wasn't even midafternoon.

Getting her rental took ages, because they had to track down her car, which wasn't in the correct parking spot. Which meant she sat in a hard chair staring at the people passing by for an hour. When she was finally given the keys, she hightailed it to the car so fast that the tiny wheels of her suitcase practically burned rubber.

Outside, the rain hadn't let up and it struck her like pins raining down. She ducked her head and made a run for it. By the time she got behind the wheel, dripping, she wondered why the hell she'd agreed to come to Wyoming.

Chapter Four

Aiden pulled up in front of the only B&B in Crossroads and cut the engine. Next to him, Hoyt hummed the song that had been on the radio. When Aiden didn't move, Hoyt nudged him.

"You getting that room for the Texas Ranger lady or what? I'm hungry and Delaney's is known to run out of chicken and biscuits on a Friday."

"I'll only be a minute."

As a courtesy, and almost an apology for the way he'd acted on that Skype call, Aiden had offered to set Amaryllis up with a room in the B&B. This way she'd arrive and be checked in. Hospitality was the least he could do, right?

The weather was mean and nasty, and she couldn't have a good flight or drive from the airport. He'd offered to pick her up, but Latchaw had informed him Amaryllis was getting a rental. He'd known she was independent and shouldn't be annoyed, but fact was, he'd been interested in seeing her next to him in his truck.

"Time's a-wastin', Roshannon," Hoyt said.

"You're welcome to go out in this downpour."

"C'mon, a rancher's kid like you, an ex-Marine, can't stand a little raindrop or two."

A wall of water hit the windshield and Aiden shot him a look. He opened the door and gave Hoyt the finger before leaping into the rain. He sprinted to the entrance and found it locked with a sign that said *Entrance on Side.*

His clothes were soaked and rivulets ran off his hat brim, but he made it into the building. Standing there dripping on their tile, he secured Amaryllis's room and paid for it with the company credit card that had been given to him to cover gasoline expenses.

The girl behind the desk couldn't be more than twenty, and she gave him a broad smile, leaning her chin on her palm. "You're mighty wet, Aiden. How about I get you a towel to dry off?"

"I'll just get wet running back to the truck. Thank you, though."

"Stay a while then. Sit down in the lounge here and watch some TV. I'll bring you a drink. Or have you had lunch yet? We serve a good hamburger."

"Uh, thanks but no. I've got the deputy waiting for me to go to Delaney's."

44

"Oh!" She opened her eyes wide. They sparkled at him. "Chicken and biscuits special. Maybe I'll come along. You got room in that truck? My mother's around and can watch the entrance."

"Um, I guess so. There's a back seat." He'd have to move some things around.

"I'll grab my umbrella."

There wasn't any use in telling her no. A second later, she appeared with a light jacket and umbrella in hand. She insisted that he share the umbrella with him, and he swore she was purposely pressing the side of her breast against his arm as he held it for them both.

When they reached the truck, Hoyt's eyebrows shot up.

Aiden gave him a shut-your-mouth look and climbed behind the wheel. Still dripping from the first run through the torrential rain. "Madison's joining us for lunch." He started the engine.

Ten minutes later Madison was cozied up next to him in a booth at Delaney's with three plates of the special on order. The young woman plastered so close to him that the wetness of his clothes had to be seeping into her dry ones. But still, she didn't move away.

When she excused herself to go to the ladies' room, Hoyt leaned across the table. "Dude, she's all over you."

"She's young." And dumb. She didn't want anything to do with him.

"And pretty. Those blue eyes are glued to you, didn't you notice?"

"No."

"Why don't you take her out? See a movie." He waggled his brows.

Madison would be sitting in his lap in a dark theater. He shook his head. "Not interested."

"What's up with you, Roshannon? You never date. You got a girlfriend somewhere we don't know about? Or are the rumors about you true and you keep one in your dungeon handcuffed to the bed?"

Alarms went off inside Aiden, along with a mental image of Amaryllis Long handcuffed to his bed. Dammit.

"No girlfriend, no dungeon."

"A sad story then? Broken heart?"

"Nope. Sorry to disappoint."

Hoyt sat back and eyed him. "Still nursing that depressed, battle-worn Marine attitude?"

"Definitely not." His words came out rough. "Just haven't found anybody worth going after."

At that moment, Madison returned, all bouncy smiles, ponytail swinging. She *was* pretty and looked limber enough for a fun romp. But that wasn't what he wanted. He needed more.

What he had in mind would scare the hell out of her.

Hoyt and Madison took up a conversation, allowing Aiden time to think... about Amaryllis and how soon she'd be in Crossroads. Rain and wind battered the front of the diner. He hoped she really had that rock-solid constitution her reputation said she did. The mountains of Wyoming could be a bitch on a good day, but in this storm, she was in for a hell of a drive.

* * * * *

Amaryllis was accustomed to small-town Podunk sheriff's offices, but this one took the prize. The building sported peeling gray paint and a front door with a dent or five that looked to be from some harsh kicks. A few small windows were set into the front, but they couldn't offer much light.

She glanced around at the vehicles in the parking lot. Same as Texas—trucks in various states of hard use. Judging by the hints of rust, most had a lot of miles on them.

She turned for the front door. Inside, a petite woman sat behind the desk, the phone pasted to her ear. When she spotted Amaryllis, her mouth dropped in an O. Moving the phone away from her ear, she said, "You must be Ms. Long."

"Amaryllis, please." She gave her a smile.

"We didn't expect you so soon. Thought you'd have a nice lie-in after that terrible drive you must have had yesterday."

"I'm fine." Amaryllis offered her a smile.

"The sheriff's out right now."

"That's okay. All I need is Roshannon."

"Well, he's flitting around here somewhere. Check his office." She pointed and Amaryllis nodded in thanks. "Nice meeting you!" the secretary called.

She raised a hand in acknowledgement and wove around office furniture to get to the space that was Aiden Roshannon's office. Closet, more like. The space barely fit a desk, a chair and a wastebasket, which was emptied. And his desk was neat with small stacks of papers in the corner and a pen cup.

No photos, no personal belongings. Nothing to show her a glimpse of the man she was going to spend her days with.

"Hello." The deep voice sent a spark of electricity through her. She turned to the doorway to find Aiden Roshannon. Taller than she'd guessed, wearing the same battered black hat he had been on their video call. His gray eyes seemed to slice through her.

A flutter in her chest had her breath catching. What the hell was that about?

"Your eye's healing."

He blinked and then a ghost of a smile touched his lips. His hard, perfect lips. A crease extended from the corner of his mouth up into his cheek. He fingered the edge of his eye. "Yep, I'm a fast healer. Should be gone by week's end."

She thrust out her hand. "Amaryllis Long."

An odd familiarity came over her. Like she'd known him much longer and not only spoken a few times on the phone or seen each other once on a computer screen. In person, he was more ruggedly handsome. Bigger. Smelled good too.

Dang, why did her body have to wake up now? It had been in a state of dormancy for months and months. Not only asleep but in a coma.

Probably because the male specimens she encountered did nothing for her.

He dropped an appraising look over her. A slow dip of his eyes from face to body that felt like a physical touch. He took her hand, enveloped it in his big, rough one, and shook it like he would a man's as he looked her in the eyes.

Exactly what she wanted — to be treated no different than any man Roshannon would meet. So why did she feel like drawing her hand free and going outside to get her bearings for a minute?

She must still have trauma from that horrible flight. No other reason for her behavior or odd thinking.

"Aiden Roshannon." Damn, the man spoke his name like the military man he'd been.

She let go of his hand and leaned back against his desk. His closeness and the small office was definitely affecting her. She thought about climbing over his desk and putting distance between them.

"How long you been working with rustlers?" she asked.

He lifted a shoulder and let it fall, making his T-shirt seem about to burst at the seams. She tried not to look at the flex of muscle — the man was stacked with it. Did the Marines have some new training regimen that layered men with an inhuman amount of muscle these days?

"Been working here little more than a year. Before that I was working with a different kind of rustler."

"Oh?"

"Yeah, ones carrying assault rifles."

"Yes, that's right." She tried to pretend she knew little of him, but why? She wasn't the type of woman to pretend ignorance on any topic. Aiden Roshannon was throwing her off balance, and she had no damn reason for it.

"And you've been with the Rangers five years."

"That's right." She sized him up. Could he handle her methods of tracking down criminals? "Well, now that we're acquainted in person, let's get straight to it." She stepped up to the door to pass through. He was close, so close she caught the piney scent coming off his body.

Aiden looked down at her, and she fought the urge to step back, to look away. Dammit, why was she reacting to him this way?

Lifting a brow, she waited for him to step aside and let her pass. He arched his brow right back at her. A heartbeat passed between them and then he moved aside, sweeping his arm toward the door in a gentlemanly gesture.

"Thanks," she muttered. Her strides couldn't be long enough to get her outside fast enough. She could use the breathing room.

"Which truck is yours?" she asked, knowing he was right behind her.

"Black one there."

One of the newer ones, well-kept with a new wax job. She tried not to be impressed by silly things like how neat he kept his office or his vehicle. She'd worked with some real slobs in her time and those things had become pet peeves for her, especially when she was climbing into the passenger seat of a dirty truck littered with fast food bags.

She strode to the truck, opened the door and climbed behind the wheel.

"What do you think you're doin'?" He stood at the door, on eye level with her, his gray eyes narrowed.

Pine scents hit her again.

"Driving," she responded.

"You don't know where you're going and we don't have a plan together yet."

"We can pull it together on the road. Besides, I've got a GPS on my phone."

He stopped short of rolling his eyes. "You don't know these parts."

She stared at him. "I was hired to do this job."

"Then get your own truck. I'm drivin', woman."

She offered him a mocking, toothy smile.

He stepped back to give her room to jump out again. While she walked around the rear of the truck, she swore she felt his gaze burning holes in her back.

Or maybe her backside?

He got in and started the truck before she was seated.

"Guess we're jumping right into work." He gripped the wheel.

"Time's a-wasting. You've got a lot of angry ranchers with their hopes pinned on you solving these cases."

She barely got her seatbelt fastened before he was backing out onto the road. She'd seen a bit of the town but hadn't ventured far in her rental car. "Where are we headed?"

"Where were you planning to go once you were behind the wheel?" He sent her a long look across the cab of the truck.

Now that she was seated next to him, she realized how overwhelming he was. It wasn't his size—there were bigger men out there. But he packed a huge Texas-style wallop. Could be a chip on his shoulder, but she'd worked with worse.

"I have some ideas where to start."

"Hmph." He pushed the sound through his chest, which seemed to rumble the airwaves throughout the truck cab. Her nipples puckered at the vibration. Damn. She stared out the windshield. What the hell was up with her body?

Recovering her brainwaves, she asked, "What's your plan, Roshannon?"

"A neighbor of one of the ranchers never seems to be home when I call. Jack Mitchell's his name. It's about time I run him to earth."

"Good start."

She didn't want to say she had the same plan in mind—to speak with the neighbor. Since nobody had any information from that man, she thought it was a little fishy. Maybe Roshannon wasn't such a newbie as she'd thought.

But that didn't make him different. Like the others she'd worked with, he didn't bother asking her ideas on the case. Well, she'd go along for the ride, for now. When they found the neighbor, she might change her mind about that.

* * * * *

54

The damn woman was as gorgeous as she'd been onscreen, and then some. Curves for miles, her hips something a man could grab onto and use to drag her down on his hard cock.

She had an air of confidence Aiden hadn't seen in the women he'd been around. Something about her seemed earthy, like she could be happy grabbing a backpack and setting out across the country on foot. At the same time, the way she held herself gave him the idea she was well-traveled. Or an Army brat.

He tried to keep his gaze from straying to her as he drove, but he was distracted as hell by those strawberry blonde waves and deep chocolate eyes. Not to mention the smattering of freckles across her nose, cheeks and forehead.

Finding her standing in his office had thrown him for a twist. He liked his space private, and nobody went in there unless invited. Then she'd gotten behind the wheel of his truck.

As if she owned it.

He worked his molars together until he felt his jaw cramp. She was a piece of work, for sure. Her believing she could drive his truck was a liberty he would not stand for.

He had no idea how to speak to a woman like Amaryllis. She sat there in silence, legs crossed in a relaxed pose, gazing out the window at the landscape as if she hadn't a care in the world and no need to make small talk with a stranger like him.

Yet he had to break the ice. He wasn't a chatty man but if they were spending long days together, he couldn't do it in complete silence. He fished around for something to say.

"Have you been to Wyoming before?"

She shook her head. "Spent about four months in Colorado last year, but I'm mostly a Southerner."

She had a lilting drawl that coiled his body into a knot.

Maybe he didn't want to hear her talking a lot, after all.

"What do you think of Wyoming?" He navigated a hairpin bend that backtracked around the mountain. The rancher experiencing the theft and neighbor they'd be speaking to owned land that backed right up against the mountain like a tail on a dog.

Amaryllis smoothed her long hair over her shoulder. "Doesn't matter what I think of Wyoming, Roshannon. I have a job to do."

"That's true." Could she be any more contrary? It was a simple question.

"Crap weather when you flew in probably didn't help your opinion of the place."

"That's true." She echoed his words. Was she mocking him? He replayed her response in his head a few times, listening for sarcasm. He didn't detect any, but that didn't mean she wasn't being... What was the word Judd had used? Intense.

Aiden fell silent, his mind sidestepping to the case. Before he could conjure a thought on it, Amaryllis spoke.

"What's the head count up to now? Nineteen cows stolen and four dead?"

"Five dead now. I was out half the night investigating it and helping the owner get the remains in a hole." His eyes still felt grainy, despite a few rounds of eyedrops. If he closed his eyes, he swore he still saw the bright headlights of his truck trained on the butchered cow.

Not butchered — slaughtered. The way they had gutted it and taken the back meat, leaving most of the cow on the road with flies buzzing around it... A damn shame. Luckily the rancher had a front-end loader and was able to dig a hole and also deposit the carcass in it without a lot of physical labor.

Amaryllis pivoted in the seat to look at him, arms folded. Eyes flashing. "You didn't fill me in on this new discovery."

"No time. You were eager to get on the road."

"You could have told me after we got in the truck."

He grunted. She was a piece of work, all right.

"Who's the owner of the latest cow killed?"

"Cole."

She pressed her lips together. "That's his second."

He had to hand it to her—she knew her stuff. He nodded. "Cole's had two killings and one theft. They did some property damage stealing the cow, broke some fence."

It was her turn to grunt, but it was the sweetest, most feminine sound he'd ever heard. It made him think of steamy summer nights rolling on hot, twisted sheets.

Or her taking his cat o'nine tails on her sweet ass.

"Typical to cut fence. But I've seen worse for property damage."

Was this a pissing match? The whole I've-seen-worse-from-cattle-rustlers-than-you-have? He wasn't entering that competition. She scooted forward in her seat. "How much farther?"

He shot her an amused glance. "Don't know these parts?"

She narrowed her brown eyes. "Of course I don't. But like I said, I can drive anywhere using a GPS."

He chuckled. "You can try, but it doesn't always work here."

She waved a hand in dismissal.

A smile tugged at his lips but he controlled his expression and kept a straight face. Last thing he wanted was for her to think he was laughing at her. Working together was going to be difficult enough.

As they drove, silence fell between them. Oddly, it wasn't entirely awkward. He could appreciate a woman who didn't feel the need to chatter and fill every spare moment. In the years since he'd been in the service, he hadn't had a regular girlfriend, but he slept with a few women after leaving the Marines. None of them were permanent girlfriend material, though a few of them had tried their hardest to keep him.

And he, Judd and his cousin Wes had spent a few months in Chicago working with a security company when Aiden was between tours. The Chicago Underground had taught them all a thing or two, and Aiden had come back with experience as a Dom and a lot of ideas about what he wanted from a relationship. That narrowed down the pool of women he was willing to date.

The road downgraded from asphalt to gravel to dirt. He took a right toward Jack Mitchell's property. He'd been here before and knew where the worst of the ruts were, so he swerved around them. Amaryllis rocked in the passenger seat, taking it all in.

From the corner of his eye, he caught the light bounce of her breasts and the way her hair swayed. He clenched his fingers around the wheel tighter. Thoughts of wrapping all that hair around his fist and yanking her head back while he cupped her full breast in his palm was *not* revolving around his head. Absolutely not. No way.

Judd and Wes would chuckle if he could hear Aiden's thoughts.

"Hold on now." The truck bumped in various potholes the size of landmines.

Amaryllis shot him a glare.

"What? I'm not doing this on purpose. Welcome to Wyoming. Where ranchers have better things to do than fill in the holes in their driveways."

"I can see working with you will be a challenge."

"Not if you can hold on tight." His crooked grin couldn't be disguised this time.

She stared at him and then shook her head but grabbed the holy-shit handle. They hit the end of the road and the ranch spread before them. Rolling land for grazing and a long house sided in rough wood. Dogs barked and chased the truck. When he rolled to a stop, the dogs leaped at the passenger window like lions lunging at prey, barking, fangs bared in greeting.

Aiden put the truck in park and sat back to see what Amaryllis would do. The few times he'd been to the property to question the owner, the dogs had tried their damnedest to run him off.

To his surprise, she opened her door and stepped out. The dogs surrounded her but she just held out her hands and let them sniff her. A snarl sounded from one, but she closed the truck door and walked off toward the house without a care.

These animals had been trained to protect their land, and they circled her like vultures on fresh meat. Amaryllis continued to walk, ignoring the hounds as she made her way forward.

He'd hand it to her—she was a tough little shit.

Aiden got out and hurried to catch up to her. One of the dogs snapped at him and he set a hand on his gun holster strapped across his hips. If one of them made a move to bite him or Amaryllis, he wouldn't stand for it.

The dogs paced around them, issuing guttural growls as they made their way onto the front porch. The place was clean, the porch free of the usual junk he saw people collect, like old tires and bits of farm equipment. About half the places he visited in these parts had toilets sitting around their front yards, some with flowers planted in the bowls but most with weeds growing around them.

Amaryllis reached the front door and raised a hand to knock. The dogs jumped around her as if she'd raised a weapon to their master, and Aiden crowded in, set to protect her.

She shot him a look.

The second rap on the door was swallowed by more sounds of snarling dogs, and Amaryllis gripped the handle and turned it.

His heart lurched. "What the hell're you doing? You can't just enter a Wyoming home without invitation or you'll meet the barrel of a shotgun."

She arched a brow at him and called, "Hello?"

A woman ran into the front room, her eyes wide at the gall of someone entering her home. She opened her mouth to speak, but the dogs were going nuts. She clapped her hand and they silenced instantly.

"Hi, I'm Amaryllis Long and this is Aiden Roshannon. We had some questions for you about the terrible crime that was committed against one of your neighbors just last night. Have you heard of it?"

The woman blinked at the sweetness of Amaryllis's voice. She sounded like she was asking after the woman's blue-ribbon-winning pickles.

Amaryllis stepped farther into the space, and the dogs reacted. Aiden reached for his .40, but Amaryllis stopped him with a touch on his forearm. Then she boldly scratched the meanest, ugliest dog between the ears. In seconds it was pushing against her hand for more.

Aiden couldn't blame it. Those fingers looked mighty tempting.

"What is your name?" Amaryllis asked the woman.

"Nicky. You can't be here."

"Special Investigator Roshannon and I work for the sheriff's department and we're asking ranchers if they've experienced any thefts on their properties. Do you have anything to report?"

The woman rubbed her palms down her thighs. Aiden watched her closely for any shiftiness in character. Her eyes held steady on Amaryllis, and he couldn't read the woman.

"I... We heard some ATVs in the woods nearby the other night. Maybe it was them."

Aiden reached for his notebook, which set the dogs to barking again. Nicky clapped to silence them, and Amaryllis tracked Aiden's movement. He flipped open the pages and set pen to paper as Nicky gave the day of the week and approximate hour.

"So you didn't find anything missing from your property after hearing the ATVs?" he asked her.

She shook her head, eyes downcast. He made note of that too and underlined it. In his years of studying people, he'd learned he could build the biggest case just by a suspect's reactions to questioning. Nicky didn't like speaking to him, that much was obvious.

"Did your husband mention anything was missing, ma'am?" Amaryllis pushed.

Her gaze flashed to Amaryllis's. "We're not married. He's been my man for four years, though."

Aiden scribbled that in his notebook without looking away from Nicky. "Where could we find your significant other? We'd like to ask if he's heard or seen anything."

"Uh, he ran into town about an hour ago."

"Could we wait for him? Will he be back soon?" Amaryllis asked.

"I'm not sure when he'll be back. I've got roast to put in the oven, though." She looked to Amaryllis, and for a crazy moment, Aiden expected Nicky to invite the woman to dinner.

"We'll come back another time, then. Thank you for talking with us." Amaryllis went to the door and the dog, now her buddy, trailed behind, nudging her hand for more ear scratching. Amaryllis patted its head in farewell and grabbed the door handle. Aiden took that as his cue they were abandoning the questioning, but he wasn't anywhere near finished.

Amaryllis stepped onto the porch and closed the door.

He looked down at her pretty face that gave away nothing of her thoughts. "She's hiding something," he said, low.

Without a word, Amaryllis headed down the porch steps and crossed the yard to the truck. The dogs were all shut up in the house, leaving it quiet enough for Aiden to think. He swung his head right and left, scoping the land for anything that seemed amiss.

Amaryllis strode toward one of the outbuildings on the property.

"You're itchin' to get yourself shot, aren't ya?" he asked, grabbing her arm. "You don't just snoop around in Wyoming."

"In Texas either, but I've never been shot yet. Come close, but the bullet missed." She spoke absently, with half a mind to her words. She was busy searching the ground.

Aiden studied the dirt where a few boot prints were set into drying mud. The heel was dug in deeper, indicating the wearer, a man judging by the size of the foot, bore his weight on his heels.

He reached for his notebook.

Amaryllis jerked her head up to stare at him. "You write everything in that?"

"Yeah. Why?"

"How cute."

He pushed out a breath, his chest hot with sudden annoyance. "How do you keep track of details?"

Her brown eyes were wide as she tapped her temple.

Aiden didn't take down his next note—to tell Judd he hadn't been kidding when he said Amaryllis Long was intense. He'd remember that just fine. The woman was a grade-A pain in the ass with neon lights flashing around her.

Too bad she set off a hundred sirens in Aiden's body.

Chapter Five

Amaryllis crouched to look at the hay scattered in front of the shed door. Aiden loomed next to her, his long denim-clad legs inches from her face, the muscles bulging in all the right spots.

"What are you looking for?" he asked.

She glanced up as he bent to examine the hay. Up close, she saw tiny creases around his eyes from squinting. And damn if the man didn't have the longest, lushest lashes imaginable. Why did guys get all the luck?

He scuffed the ground with the toe of his boot. "Looks like hay to me."

"Thank you, Sherlock. I can see that. I was looking for blood. If I lived here, I'd hang some meat in this shed that's closest to the house."

He straightened and she unfolded from her crouch. Their gazes met. "We'll come back with a search warrant."

"I'd just open the door and look." She put her hand on the doorknob and twisted.

He poked his head inside, and she pushed closer to see too. The inside was dim, musty, but only held some farming implements.

Aiden dragged in a deep breath, and Amaryllis froze. Was he... sniffing her? She chanced a look at him, but he was still staring into the dark interior.

Dumb. He's sniffing the shed to see if meat was hung in here.

"You satisfied that this is just an old shed?" Aiden asked.

"Yes." She stepped away—far away. She didn't want to admit to the surge of sensations she felt when he was close to her. And earlier, when he'd put a hand on her arm, had he felt that electricity too?

She must have lost her mind back at ten-thousand feet during that turbulence. Because she was not a woman who drooled over men, and especially not ones as guarded as Roshannon.

They headed to the truck. Just as they reached it, Nicky unleashed the hell hounds and they launched off the porch, running full tilt for her and Aiden.

"Get in the truck," he snapped to her.

Was he seriously ordering her around? She narrowed her eyes at him, and to be contrary, she turned to watch the dogs race at her. She held out her hand, and one of the meaner ones lunged forward. Her heart stuck in her throat but she managed not to jerk her hand and cause it to react by biting. Remaining calm, aware Aiden was glaring holes in her, she spoke to the dogs as she opened the door. She managed to wiggle into the truck and pull the door shut, closing out the snarling beasts with canines bared.

"You must enjoy taking risks more than I thought. Those dogs were ready to make you their supper." Aiden sounded grumpier than a treed coon.

"They aren't that bad."

He gaped at her. "Are you serious?"

"Well, the one cozied up to me after a few minutes."

He pushed out a breath through his nostrils and started the truck. Without looking behind him, he backed up. Dogs scattered and chased after the tires.

"There's a reason these dogs are so mean," Aiden said.

She swung her gaze his way. "What? Are they abused? I'll have animal control up here so fast to take them away that—"

"No, not abused. They're mean because their owner's mean. That woman of his is cowed, couldn't you tell? She's hiding him, and I don't like it."

"So get a warrant to search the place like you said."

"Why do I need a warrant when you can just barge into the house without knocking?"

"Are we back on this topic again?" She rolled her eyes and folded her arms. "In this business, you've got to take risks, Roshannon."

"Risking that you could be shot isn't my idea of by the book," he muttered.

She dug her fingers into the edge of the seat, holding on as he navigated the bumpy drive. She wasn't going to give Aiden the satisfaction of seeing her hold on to the handle.

"Is that how you operate, Roshannon? By a code of rules? Most cases are solved by dumb, blind luck. You open a door and catch someone in the act."

"Of what? Loading shells into his shotgun?"

She pressed her lips together. "I'm surprised you didn't write that in your notebook yet."

He made a noise in his throat, and very pointedly removed the notebook from his pocket, along with his pen. He shoved the end of the pen against his front teeth, clicking it into position to write. Then he mashed the book to the steering wheel and scrawled something across the pages that looked suspiciously like *Long is a pain.*

"Stop the truck and let me drive if you're gonna be scribbling down your grocery list." She reached for the wheel. He dropped the notebook into his lap and gripped her fingers in his big, warm, callused hand.

Liquid heat traveled through her limbs and pooled in her belly. She yanked her hand back and stared out the windshield, fuming at him. And herself for letting him get to her. She didn't understand what was going on, but it had to be blind, ignorant attraction.

She definitely wouldn't cross any lines with Roshannon, though. They were work colleagues, period. Even if it looked like the threads on his shirt were popping from the mere flex of his biceps just for her viewing pleasure.

"Let's get one thing straight and we can deal with each other, Amaryllis." God, did his voice have to be deep and rich with a hint of gravel?

She tangled her hands in her lap and set her jaw for a fight. "Name your terms."

"Hands off my truck."

"What is it with men and their trucks? You'd swear it's their manhood, a set of balls or something."

Was the corner of his mouth tugging upward? Couldn't be. He had to be struggling with gas or something. Served him right. She hoped he got stomach cramps.

"Around these parts, a man's truck can mean survival, so yeah, we're pretty protective of our assets." He drawled the last word in a way that made her think he *was* referring to his balls.

"Fine, hands off the truck. But I do know how to drive, and pretty well if I do say so myself."

"I have no doubts you can do whatever you put your mind to, Ms. Long. But I'd appreciate if you didn't pull another stunt like you did back there either." He jerked his thumb over his shoulder.

She saw a hint of shadows moving within the depths of his gray eyes. Stormy eyes. Like the damn Wyoming weather. "What are you referring to?"

"Lordy, woman, you know damn well I mean you opening that door and walking right into what could have been a very bad situation."

"And I told you that sometimes you have to look in places without asking first. Damn, I bet you did everything your momma wanted you to with a thank you, ma'am."

He glared at her.

"Nothing happened. We got a little bit of information from that woman. I do think her 'man' is involved in stealing or butchering some of the cattle around here, but I don't believe he's the only one. I think there's a group. Going separate ways, committing separate crimes to throw us off."

He grew solemn and stared out at the road he'd just turned onto. In the near distance, mountains rose up, stark and jagged into the gray sky. The cut of Aiden Roshannon's jaw wasn't much different from the harsh lines of the landscape. He seemed to have sprouted more stubble in the last hour since she'd met him, too.

"Well?" she said after a long silence that followed. "What do you think of my theory?"

"I think it's so close to mine that I'm scared."

At that, she burst out laughing. She couldn't help it. The notion of him being afraid of her amused and delighted her in ways she couldn't begin to describe. Maybe she really was a ball-buster like her daddy claimed.

Nah, she wasn't one of those crazy feminist types. She just wanted to be treated as an equal, and come hell or high water, she'd get that from Aiden Roshannon.

"We're sharing insights on a crime, Roshannon. Not a brain."

74

"Thank God for that." He shot her a look and there it was—a crooked grin only a true country boy could manage.

Damn, there went her libido again, like a swelling wave rising upward.

She chuckled and dug around in her pocket for a pack of gum. She took a piece and offered the pack to Aiden. He shook his head. "I need something more than gum to hold me over. I haven't eaten in about eighteen hours, and if I don't get something soon, you're not going to like me very much."

"Wow, you mean you can get grumpier?"

He issued a low growl that only managed to make her feel hot and sweaty again.

"We need to keep on this trail. The crime's still fresh."

He whipped into a little diner along the road. "So are the eggs here at Delaney's." He parked between two other trucks and cut the engine. "C'mon."

He climbed out and slammed the door before she could think of a retort about work ethics. She had no choice but to follow him inside. Once the scent of grease and frying bacon hit her, she realized her stomach had finally recovered from the airsickness that had seemed to hover over her long after the flight had ended. She was starving.

Without a backward glance, Aiden strolled to one of the booths, tugging the brim of his hat in greeting to everyone he passed.

He slid into the booth and she took a seat across from him. Okay, this was weirdly intimate, like a date.

"Don't look so uptight, Amaryllis. It's just breakfast."

"I'm not used to eating at this hour."

"Then get coffee." He opened the laminated menu and ignored her as he made his choice.

When she didn't open her own menu, he glanced up at her, gaze direct. "We can't run around these parts all day without eating anything. When you see an opportunity to stop, you'd better take it because it could be eighteen more hours before you get a chance to."

She opened the menu and her stomach rumbled at the selection of food that wouldn't do anything for her arteries or the way her skinny jeans fit. But when the waitress came, Aiden gestured for Amaryllis to order first. She got a breakfast sampler with one scrambled egg, homemade sausage, two pancakes and a side of fresh fruit.

"I'll have the Mountain Man," Aiden said, flipping his menu shut. "And a pot of coffee."

"I know you like it strong, Aiden. Be right back with your coffee." The waitress dropped a wink and moved off.

Aiden centered his attention on Amaryllis. She concentrated on relaxing her shoulders and fighting the urge to bolt to the ladies' room to escape his stare.

"You love your job." His simple statement caught her off guard.

She nodded. "Yes."

"And it's your life."

It was, but did admitting it make her sound sort of lonely and desperate? Like those women who devoted their time to cat charities?

"I guess you could say that," she said.

"It's mine too. But I can't let you go storming into any more houses on an empty stomach." His lips curved up slightly in what might be a smile. Or maybe it really was gas.

A cowboy stopped by the booth to speak with Aiden, and she tried to look at her new partner without seeming like she was staring. The guy asked about some of the rumors that Hanson had another cow killed and Aiden confirmed his story with as little information as possible.

Amaryllis listened for a minute and when the conversation lulled, she thrust out her hand toward the man. "I'm Amaryllis Long."

The forty-something guy cocked his head and gave her a closer look. "Why, I'll be damned. You are. You're famous around these parts. Roshannon, is she working with you?"

"I am," she answered for herself.

"I'm probably interrupting some important talk about the case. I'll leave you be. But I'll know where to look you up if I have any cattle stolen." He dropped his gaze to Amaryllis's breasts.

"I doubt you'll find any cattle in my top, sir. Thanks for stopping by."

Aiden spit out his coffee. The man moved away, a blush around his ears. Grabbing a handful of napkins from the dispenser on the table, Aiden mopped at the mess he'd made.

"My God, woman, you don't hold anything back, do you?"

"I've learned it doesn't really do much good." She sighed and added a dash of cream to her cup.

Just then the waitress brought their platters. Amaryllis barely glanced at the one put before her because Aiden's was indeed something only a mountain man could eat.

Piled high with every breakfast food available. There was no way he could eat that.

Five minutes later, she doubted her prediction. He'd already worked through his hotcakes and polished off his sausage. He bit off a piece of bacon and it was impossible not to gawk at the way his angled jaw moved as he chewed. A slight film of grease on his lips only made him appear hotter.

She turned to her sliced melon and cut off a piece. It tasted pale in comparison to the hearty fried food.

"Not a lot of good seasonal produce up this way. Best to stick with anything Delaney can put on the griddle."

"I just discovered that. The food's great." If Aiden ate this way all the time, he must spend every spare moment of his free time at the gym.

He nodded and swallowed the rest of his bacon. He was still eating when she sat back, full, to sip her coffee.

He poured more into his mug and drank it black. He cocked his head and focused on her face, but he wasn't really looking at her. She opened her mouth to ask what he was doing when she overheard a conversation from a booth behind them. Talk about cattle and how a cattle auction three hours west of here had added a second day because they'd had such a big influx of cattle for market.

Amaryllis set down her mug and Aiden waved to the waitress. In less than a minute, they were on the road, headed west.

Chapter Six

Aiden's momma always said that sharing a meal with someone made you friends. He wouldn't go that far with Amaryllis, but she didn't look as uncomfortable riding next to him as she had before their stop at the diner.

He was glad of it—he couldn't take hours on the road with her sitting like she had a stick up her ass.

She sat relaxed, legs crossed, fiddling with her phone. "There isn't very good service up here, is there?"

"Only service you'll get in some of these parts is a commune with God." He glanced at the sky, still a foggy gray from the line of storms that had come in earlier in the week.

They were an hour into the three-hour drive and it was dragging. Maybe because he didn't know if he should turn on the radio to pass the time the way he always did. Or it could be the fact his gaze kept straying to her crossed thighs.

Her skinny jeans accentuated the lines of muscle. He opened his mouth to ask if she was a runner but thought better of it. She'd know he was looking at her legs.

Suddenly his Wranglers were a little too tight. No denying she was a beautiful woman, but there was something that sucked him in and made him want to know more.

Like how breathy her voice got when he was moving inside her.

And when she was tied spread-eagle on his bed.

He wasn't going to lie to himself that he didn't want her that way—the dirtiest, darkest way possible. That he didn't want to have her bound hand and foot, the complex knots creating the perfect lingerie against her pale body.

Sexually, he hadn't played that way in a long time, and his cock was all too happy at the thought.

Aiden looked across the cab. Her head was bent, thick hair cascading over her shoulder and down to her breast. He knotted his fist on his thigh to keep from reaching over and seeing if her strawberry blonde locks were as silky as they appeared.

She abandoned her phone with a heavy sigh.

"Are you trying to text someone?" Maybe she had a boyfriend. He didn't know much about her other than she was impulsive, had a smart mouth and a great ass.

"I was trying to get a list of the breeders going to auction today. I wanted to see the cattle brands. I may have to contact a friend of mine who's a brand investigator down South."

"Would he know the brands up this way? It's a big country with a lot of ranchers. I have the local brands here in my notebook." He removed it from his pocket.

She grabbed it from his hand. He watched her slender fingers move over the cover and then flip through pages.

"You're meticulous, I'll give you that, Roshannon."

In all things. Wait till you see how I place the stripes of my whip on your ass.

He jerked straighter in his seat, resisting the urge to adjust his dick.

"What's this?" She ran her fingertip down a page, over the heavy black ink of his writing.

"I can't exactly read it from here." Why were his balls aching just from watching her finger touch the pages of his notebook?

"Lime. Shovel." She peered more closely at the scribbled text. "Does this say honey?"

He chuckled. "You're reading my shopping list."

She gaped at him. "Are you burying a body and then having honey on your toast?"

"Nah, that's stuff for my ranch."

She blinked at him. "You own a ranch?"

"My family does. My pa still runs things, but sometimes he calls up me or my twin brother to run some errands." Wes was always on the road and too busy to run for supplies.

"And you needed honey for…?" Her brown eyes seemed to glow with mischief.

His cock hardened to full mast in that one look. "My momma asked for it." It was damn wrong for a man to have to speak of his mother when he had a hard-on for a beautiful woman, but Amaryllis made him anything but comfortable. He didn't imagine *anything* about her was easy.

"I knew it." Amaryllis laughed, a low, sweet tone that sharpened the edge of his need. The next two hours of their drive were going to be damn difficult unless she sprouted hair all over her body and shriveled into an ugly old woman.

Hell, even then she'd still have that air of confidence that was sexy as fuck.

"And did you get your momma the honey she asked for? What was she making?"

"Cinnamon rolls, as I recall. My brother's favorite."

"But they're not your favorite?"

"No. I like apple pie." And the taste of a sweet, wet pussy. He ran his tongue over his lips and focused on a point on the horizon. This was going downhill in a hurry. If he didn't get hold of his raging hormones, he'd have to pull over at the first rest stop and relieve himself of a load of sperm.

"Your twin and you have different favorites?" She directed a lock of hair behind her ear, which only made him harder. The shell inviting nibbles, licks and bites. Her lobe was pierced with a single silver horseshoe-shaped stud.

"Contrary to popular belief, twins don't do everything the same."

"But you're identical. I saw a picture of you."

So she'd stalked him.

"We are identical, but we're still two people."

"Name some of your differences." The spark of intelligence in her eyes and the eagerness to learn something new, even if it was about him and his twin, lit up her face with a glow.

He had a hard time keeping his eyes on the road. She made a sober man feel drunk. "When we were babies, I loved taking baths and he screamed the whole time." He swung a look her direction to find her smiling.

"What else?"

"I went to the military and he stayed back to help on the ranch."

"Was that difficult to be separated from him?"

"No more than any other family member. Though, sometimes…" He broke off, wondering if she'd think he was nuts if he told her about his and Judd's innate sense of each other. Their connection that felt like a live wire when the other was in trouble. It was how Judd had first known about Aiden's trouble overseas. After Judd had gotten a whiff of that, he'd found out what flight he was on and met him on base. He'd been there for Aiden during the questioning, though he wasn't allowed to be present.

There were times Aiden's link with Judd didn't end well. Like the time he rushed home to find his girlfriend with her arms around Judd, her lips superglued to his.

After that, they hadn't spoken for three months. Aiden had been headed to the Marines anyway and Judd had sworn she'd kissed *him*. But Aiden had been glad he had someplace to go to gain some distance between him and his brother. Having his ass kicked at boot camp had been exactly what he needed to forget the whole event.

He also shared a connection of sorts with Wes. They might not be twins but they had the same tastes—in women and what they wanted from them. Which was how they'd ended up passing Lorna back and forth between them that summer before he'd left for boot camp. She had been more than willing, and Aiden found sharing the burden of a woman's needs easier than dealing with her on his own. If he didn't feel up to it, Wes took her out to dinner and pampered her.

He focused on Amaryllis. She was nothing like Lorna. Yet she had a ripe sexuality about her that made Aiden wonder...

She waited for him to say more on the topic of the link with his twin.

"Sometimes we just know when the other needs us. You probably think I'm crazy."

She shook her head. "I've read about things like that. Tell me about one time."

He pressed his lips together and thought on it. He wasn't about to tell her about his time in the Marines.

The road stretched before them, and they had plenty of time to get to know each other. So why was he only thinking of finding out what her naked body looked like?

"When we were ten, Judd started hanging out with this kid from school. I never liked the punk, but Judd said he was a nice guy when other kids weren't around. He went back to his friend's place with him after school one day and I went on home. About seven o'clock I started getting this bad feeling." He shifted his shoulders, that crawling sensation overcoming him all over again.

Amaryllis twisted in her seat, legs drawn up and to the side, listening to his story.

"I didn't know what was wrong with me, but I told my mother I didn't feel well and she dosed me with Pepto Bismol. But it didn't do any good. By eight o'clock I felt like my skin would burst. I just knew I had to go find Judd. I made the excuse I was checking on my new pony and ran straight to Judd's friend's house. When I got there, I don't know what made me look up into the trees, but there he was, stuck high in the branches, too scared to come down."

"Oh no." Amaryllis's whispered word tore through Aiden.

"The jerk friend of his had bet him who could climb higher and then Judd was on an unsteady branch and his buddy climbed down and left him there."

"Oh my God."

"He'd been sitting in the tree for hours, and when he saw me, he started crying." Aiden's voice was thick.

"What did you do?"

"Climbed the tree and guided him down."

"And Judd's friend?"

"Next day Wes and I cornered the kid outside school and let Judd rough him up. After that, we sort of stuck to ourselves. The three of us had some friends in school but we kept it tight. We all grew up on the ranch, lived under one roof."

"Your cousin too?"

He nodded. "His dad was out of the picture and his mom ran off. Don't know many mothers who leave their kids, but she must have had her reasons."

"You never found them out?" she asked.

He shook his head. "Times were hard. Probably figured my parents would do a better job raising a baby, seein' how they had a home and steady income."

"That must have felt like growing up with two brothers."

"Definitely. We're close. Still meet up at least once a month on the ranch for dinner or to stay the weekend and put up hay."

She smiled and sat back in her seat. "Sounds like my family. I've got two older brothers." She looked like she wanted to say more but didn't. After a long minute, she said, "I could use a drink. Is there someplace to stop?"

He threw a half-smile her way. "There's water in a cooler in the back. I'll pull over so we can get some out. Told ya there aren't many stopping points around here."

"I'm glad we ate when we did then."

He pulled off the road and got out. The breeze whispered through the high grasses alongside the asphalt as he walked to the back and reached into the cooler. With two bottled waters in hand, he started back to the driver's side.

Something made him circle to Amaryllis's side.

His boots crunched gravel at the roadside as he opened her door. She looked up in surprise. He moved close, and she reached for a bottle. When he passed it to her, their fingers brushed. Electricity zapped up his arm, shooting with lightning speed through the rest of his body. Pressure built in his groin.

Their gazes met. It wasn't the first time he'd felt that sensation when he touched her. Earlier, when he'd grabbed her arm, his knees had nearly buckled. He chalked it up to worry about her barging into that home. Now, he wasn't so sure.

He uncapped his water and raised it to his lips, watching her from hooded eyes do the same. The way she pursed her lips against the bottle and the movement of her throat as she swallowed shouldn't smack a man with lust this way.

When she lowered the drink, she gave him a long, appraising look. Her hair glinted red-gold, completely at odds with her dark brown eyes. Her plump lips, without a hint of lipstick, called for deep kisses and gasping cries of pleasure.

He found himself stepping closer. "We've got a couple more hours. You good?"

She nodded. Her gaze seemed to be fixed to his jaw. Then she flicked her eyes up and met his stare.

Fuck, it *was* there—that deep attraction that he needed from a woman to gain her complete trust. Which led them both down the slippery slope to his raw hungers, a dark room and a safe word.

Did she feel the stirring too? He had no way of knowing what was going on behind those beautiful baby browns. She bit down on her lower lip, spiking his need more.

"We'd best get on the road. I want to look at your notebook for those brands, too." Her words cut into the moment, reminding him that he could not start this up right now.

"Yep. On the road." He stepped back and closed her door, draining his water and tossing the empty bottle into the truck bed as he rounded to his door. Two hours to go.

Two hours he had to sit there with a woody thinking about binding Amaryllis's pale white wrists together and kissing every inch of her sweet, curvy body.

* * * * *

If she'd seen one cattle auction, she'd seen them all. Amaryllis folded her arms over her chest and surveyed the sea of cowboy hats. Her mind worked at record pace, taking in the cowboys' body language one at a time. She'd taken down enough rustlers that she knew what to look for.

Shadiness was number one in her book. The guys who didn't speak to the others, who stood off on their own. She'd long ago learned that ranching was a solitary business and ranchers were accustomed to working alone. But when they got a chance to shoot the shit about cattle, they took it.

Second on her list was anybody who looked out of place. Jeans that were too nice or any jacket besides a Carhartt attracted her attention. Back in Texas, she'd seen plenty of city folk trying to pass themselves off as ranchers, but their designer clothing gave them away if their polished grooming didn't.

Aiden appeared at her elbow, standing so close his body heat waved over her. It made her clothing seem thin and useless. Under her plaid top and jeans, her skin prickled.

She threw a glance at him. Damn, had his beard sprouted even more in the ten minutes he'd been away from her? His jaw was shadowed with stubble that seemed to be darkening by the second.

His attention was on the crowd as well, and she'd love to hear his thoughts. If he knew hers, he'd be grabbing her and slamming his mouth over hers, not scribbling in that notebook of his.

"Auction'll start in a few minutes," he said.

"Time enough for us to inspect brands. Let's go." Without waiting for his response, she turned and dived into the crowd. She had to nudge her way through all the broad shoulders, and more than a few men tipped their hats to her.

"Hey, sugar."

A growl sounded behind her, and she tossed a look over her shoulder to see Roshannon pushing his way after her.

"What can I do for you, honey? Are you looking for the little girls' room?" a cowboy asked as she moved by.

She narrowed her eyes at him. She wasn't a little girl and she sure as hell wasn't only here looking to find a toilet. Hot words lay on her tongue, but she gulped them down and kept walking.

When she reached the back where all the corrals were located, she fished in her back pocket for her ID. A brick wall of a man was obviously standing guard, and she flashed her badge at him.

"Special Ranger Amaryllis Long. I'd like to have a look at the cattle."

The man blinked down at her, a befuddled smile on his face. Amaryllis's pulse pounded in her temples. She didn't want to bust this guy's balls but she would if he didn't stop looking at her like she was only good for looking pretty.

An arm, lightly furred, extended next to her face with another ID. "Roshannon."

The guard swung his stare to Aiden standing behind her. "She with you?"

"No," Amaryllis snapped. "*He's* with *me*. Thank you very much." She breezed by the guy, battling the urge to kick his shins with the sharp little toes of her boots. She mumbled under her breath.

"What was that?" Aiden's tone said he knew exactly how ticked off she was to be treated lesser, to be put below him.

"Watch yourself, Roshannon."

"Why? Do you know Kung Fu? Are you gonna take me and that guard back there out?"

She paused to give him a once-over. "The guard for sure. You're pushing your luck, but I'll give you another chance. I need your help. Get out your book."

She'd memorized many of the brands, but he had several pages of them drawn in a careful hand.

He opened the notebook to the exact page as if he practiced it on a daily basis. Probably did. She huddled close to inspect the drawings.

"Got it?" he asked, his head bent close.

Pine and man. Dammit, why couldn't she stop noticing these things about him?

"Yes." She moved to the corral where a group of a dozen black angus crowded. She reached between the bars and smacked one on the rump to move it around to the side where she could see the brand.

"Two Forks," Aiden said beside her.

"Not on the list of cattle we're looking for."

"Nope."

On some level searching the auction for stolen cattle was like finding kidnapped persons. The animals were just as vulnerable, and the people who wanted them back just as desperate. Which was what made her job—and Aiden's—so important.

The next group Aiden identified right away. They moved on to the next and the next. She kept her eye on the cattle in the pens and various chutes waiting to go on the auction block, but also on the men milling around the area.

One kept glancing at her, which wasn't anything new. Weren't many women that came to auctions. The occasional rancher's wife. But Amaryllis stuck out like pink unicorn.

She'd tried wearing her hair in a ponytail and baggy tops to disguise her curves. But it hadn't taken long to realize she was going to be recognized for what she did for ranchers and not what she looked like.

"Hey, sweetheart. You look mighty familiar," one guy called out.

Aiden slowed his steps, his gaze trained on the man. Aiden's arms might be swinging loosely at his sides, but they ended in fists. He adopted a slow, predatory roll to his walk, and she imagined he'd used it quite a bit during his years in the military.

"What's your name, sweetheart?" The guy ignored Aiden and tried to get her attention.

She kept walking, aware that Aiden wasn't following. She did a mental eye-roll. She didn't have time for chest-thumping males. She'd worked with enough of them to know men would be men. They claimed top spots as friends or work colleagues and they didn't like to be pushed out.

She groaned and left them to sort their differences while she edged up to a trailer. It held just four beasts, some young bulls by the looks of them. Two of the Owens' bulls and one other had gone missing in the past two weeks. In her experience, thieves usually waited a few weeks before turning the animals at auction.

If they were smart, anyway.

She went right up to the trailer, catching sight of a fresh weal on the side of one bull. A brand over a brand.

A guy eyed her from about ten paces away, and she kept him in her radar as she tried to see the second bull's brand. It wouldn't move enough for her to get a good look without boarding the trailer. Far too dangerous. She didn't want to be crushed in a small space by thousands of pounds of flesh.

"Back off, asshole," she heard Roshannon say.

Just as she spotted the fresh brand on the next rump.

97

She looked up at the guy. He slid his eyes down and to the side as he turned slightly away.

Shadiness? Check, motherfucker.

She started toward him. "Hey, these your animals?"

He took a big step back, not forward like a man selling cattle would do if asked. Wait— was he sporting a ball cap with a brand on it— same as the newly scorched ones of the cattle she'd seen?

"You need to open the trailer and let me have a look at them." Command sounded in her tone.

Behind her, she caught a low *thump* and a grunt of pain. Either someone had just gotten kicked by a rogue hoof or Roshannon was involved in a fight. *Let's hope it's this cattle thief's cronies. AND that Aiden doesn't get another black eye.*

"What do you know about those double-branded cattle?" Roshannon barked.

A scuffling noise as the man he questioned obviously tried to make a run for it.

"On your knees, hands up."

A *thud.*

She had her sights trained on the man before her, the one looking right and left as if searching for escape. "Get on your knees," she called to the man.

"Your woman's got a... great ass," the man Roshannon was handling said. Several thumps and grunts followed, and the man in front of her took off.

She lunged forward, relying on her speed and years of chasing greased pigs at the county fair as a kid. She threw herself at him and struck with a body-shaking blow. They fell to the ground, rolling. He jerked a shoulder back, bashing her own. Pain ricocheted up into her neck.

She had enough experience under her silver belt buckle to use her wits. She ground a knee into his spine and used her weight to pin him as she got her handcuffs around one of his wrists.

He fought. He was strong, she'd give him that, and mad. But she was madder.

"Jesus Christ!" Roshannon's deep tone reached her just as she managed to hook the guy's second wrist into the cuffs.

She sat atop him, breathing hard. Her hat had been knocked off in the fall and her hair dangled into one eye. Aiden's gray gaze met hers.

"Hell, Amaryllis."

"At least two stolen animals in that trailer over there." She jerked her head and fresh pain hit the muscles of her neck. She'd definitely be sore later. The man she was sitting on was no lightweight and that jerk of his shoulder had been the equivalent of being hit by a smart car at least.

On the ground a few yards away lay the guy Roshannon had cuffed, his hat fallen off, his face scraped and what Amaryllis figured was a black eye from Roshannon's fist after the comment about her ass.

"Hey, I've been a bad boy too. Cuff me!" called a cowboy to her left where a group was gathering.

Amaryllis pushed off the guy and he groaned.

Aiden moved so fast that he was a blur. He went from a crouch to a full stand and twisted at the same second. He took two steps toward the group of guys, who were talking among themselves about who would get cuffed next by the pretty cowgirl.

"Shut your mouths and show some respect," Aiden ordered.

"Let's get these two into the truck fast in case there are others. We don't want them to find out what happened to their buddy." Amaryllis spoke close to his ear.

He gave a stiff nod, which was better than she could do. Her neck was really hurting. He bent and gripped the guy she'd just caught by the scruff and hauled him to his feet.

"Hey, what'd he do? Is hitting on you against the law, sweetheart?" one guy called.

Amaryllis flashed her ID, which silenced the group. "He's wanted for questioning. That's all you need to know." She stomped up to the other guy and nudged him in the leg with the toe of her boot. "Get up."

Without the use of his hands, he struggled, and Amaryllis had to assist him. She passed him off to the guard who was looking at her with a bit more respect now.

Aiden shoved his guy forward into a walk. While he and the guard whisked the men out of sight, she got the trailer open and shooed the cattle out. Sure enough, two fit the description of Owens' stolen cows. Judging by the crisscross of two lines, the original brand was Owens' too. He'd be happy to get a few of his animals back, and the others might be somewhere around here.

She waved at a cowboy working the auction to help her get the animals corralled into a safe place while she made a call. "Latchaw, send Owens up here with a trailer to collect two of his cattle."

"You found them? Holy shit."

101

"Yeah, and we're sending two guys to the local station for questioning. If Aiden lets them live that long." When he'd looked at the man Amaryllis had struggled with, his expression had scared even her. Cold, calculating fury. The gray of his eyes turned to steel. She didn't want to be on the receiving end of his anger, but she sure as hell wanted to hear him unleash it on that asshole.

She got off the phone with Latchaw and spoke to the market inspector. She ordered him to have every single animal unloaded for her to look at before the auction began.

Then she headed off to find her partner, feeling stiff as hell but satisfied. Aiden had the guys at the truck. One in the back seat cuffed to a length of chain connected to the door. And the other at the tailgate with a similar bit of chain.

She cocked her brow in question.

"Tire chains. For bad weather. Guess you don't have them in Texas."

"Seems like they come in handy."

They stared at each other. While she was dusty from her roll in the dirt, feeling disheveled and bruised, Roshannon managed to look like he'd just stepped off the pages of *Cowboy Magazine*.

"You got your man, Amaryllis." Aiden's voice was rougher than usual but when she looked at his face, he was wearing a smile.

She circled the truck to speak to both guys they had in custody. "Some women like diamonds and pearls. But I love seeing my metal cuffs on the wrists of a rustler. So shiny." She shot each of them a wink and heard Aiden's low rumble of amusement.

* * * * *

Aiden didn't know if he'd recover anytime soon over the jolt to his heart when he'd seen Amaryllis and the rustler hit the ground rolling. She was tiny, and this guy wasn't a tanked-up Marine, but he had some weight on him and he hadn't held back in their fall.

She'd been steamrollered and Aiden'd seen her head knocked aside. She hadn't blinked an eye before she'd gotten the man down in the dirt, her knee in his back.

What Aiden wouldn't give to have her sitting atop him. Damn.

Part of him was seething that she hadn't waited for his backup before calling out the guy. He'd tried to run, and that had to mean he was guilty of some crime, even if it wasn't stealing cattle.

And part of Aiden was proud as hell of her.

Maybe he'd tell her that right after he got done telling her off for not playing by the rules. There had to be order to making an arrest, but she was impulsive. Reckless, even.

She wouldn't listen to him. He didn't think she knew how to think before she acted. Twice now he'd seen her take careless steps. One of these times she'd end up in trouble for it. He just hoped to hell he was there to protect her when it happened.

Speaking of protection… He wasn't so sure she wasn't a walking victim with a bulls-eye on her back. She attracted attention wherever she went. Men couldn't keep their damn grubby eyeballs off her. Hell, the guy he'd knocked around had muttered about taking her sweet little ass for his own as she walked away. And then there were the ones who'd asked her to cuff them.

Fuck. Aiden wanted to sink his fist into an eye socket or two right now.

The local sheriff had their suspect in the back seat of his cruiser. He approached Aiden and Amaryllis. "We got this, Roshannon, Ms. Long. We'll be in touch with you later. Will you be sticking around town? Be happy to spot you a beer." He was an older guy who was buddies with Judd and often exchanged favors with him. Aiden had no doubt his brother would be hearing about this—and Amaryllis's role in catching the guy.

"Thank you, Sheriff Mead, but we'll be heading back to Crossroads." Her casual stance, arms crossed, exuded that air of confidence that had Aiden's cock sitting up and begging every time.

But he still wanted to turn her over his knee and paddle her ass for scaring the fuck out of him.

"Thank you for your help, Sheriff. We'll be by the station later to ask him some questions," Aiden said.

The sheriff took his leave with a parting, "Say hello to Judd for me."

"Will do." Aiden tugged his hat brim in farewell.

He and Amaryllis watched the sheriff drive away.

Aiden rounded on her and caught her by the arm. She gasped, eyes wide. "Dammit, you should have waited for me."

She tugged free and moved her hand to her neck. Pain creased her brow before she dropped her hand.

"You're hurt."

"Am not. Why should I have waited for you anyway? I've done this a time or two hundred, Roshannon."

He kept getting flashes of her rolling under that fucker, and he was getting riled again. He really needed to punch something now.

"We have ways of doing things around here, Amar—"

She cut him off. "And I have ways of doing things of my own. Just because I didn't consult a notebook before taking action doesn't mean I did it wrong. I got the job done. Isn't that the objective?"

He dragged in a full breath and counted to ten before releasing it. "There is a reason that rules are put into place. So people don't get hurt."

"I'm not hurt. Are you hurt? Oh yeah, your knuckles are bleeding. Why did you punch that guy, anyway?"

He ground his molars together, burning to grab her and silence that sassy mouth of hers with a kiss. "Shutting someone up is different than apprehending a suspect alone when he outweighs you by a hundred pounds."

"I didn't find it a problem." She examined her fingernails and rubbed at one perfect oval-shaped nail with her forefinger. "Oh, I did get a small chip in my clear coat. Guess I'd better head over to the beauty shop and get a mani. Maybe put on a pretty dress and pantyhose too."

"I know what you're doing, Amaryllis. You know damn well we're not having this discussion because you're female. If they'd sent me a male partner who acted this way, barging into houses unasked and unannounced and hurling themselves at big guys—"

She spun and walked away from him, unwilling to listen to a laundry list of her supposed broken rules. If he wanted to play some boring game of chess, let him. She wasn't here to be nice—she was here to catch cattle thieves.

Her long strides ate up the distance between Aiden and the cattle. One by one, she inspected them before letting them go to auction. After a few cows, she felt Aiden at her side, checking along with her. He didn't speak and she had nothing to say.

When they were finished, they watched the auction. It went long into the evening. By then, Owens showed up to collect his stolen bulls. Which meant standing around talking specifics for an hour or so. By the time they wrapped up, she was ready to call it quits for the day.

"Think it's worth sticking around for day two of the auction?" she asked Aiden. She didn't exactly like the silence or tension between them. He'd hardly spoken a word or glanced her direction since telling her off for breaking the rules.

"That rustler might not be the only one in town. Coulda gotten wind of what went down here today and will run scared. But maybe not. He could be arriving tomorrow. We need to stay in town and be here bright and early in the morning."

"I agree."

"At least we agree on somethin'."

So, he was going to be stubborn about things. She'd had a hell of a long day with him, and for a first day on the job together, they'd argued a lot. But it would soon be over. They'd get rooms in town and she could sink into a hot bath and soak her sore neck muscles and the bruise she felt rising on her hip. Plus, she was starving.

"Let's get outta here." He twitched his head in the direction of the parking lot.

They grabbed a bite to eat at the pizza joint, and she was so hungry that she wasn't even embarrassed to pig out. "I can see why you had that big platter this morning."

A man of few words, he only nodded and tucked into his third slice of deep dish pepperoni. After their meal, they stopped at the only two motels in town and learned they had no vacancies because of the auction. "We've got one more option," he said, hopping behind the wheel.

They drove a short distance up the road and down a long lane to a bed and breakfast. She offered to go check on the rooms, but he jumped out and practically ran into the quaint home with cabin-like details. She couldn't ignore the feeling he wanted to get rid of her for the night, and quick. Well, the feeling was mutual. He was arrogant. He had a stick up his ass when it came to rules. And his beard had grown in entirely too much during the course of the day, leaving him looking dastardly and sexy as hell.

She rubbed at the sore spot on her neck but as soon as he yanked the door open, she dropped her hand to her lap. She didn't want him to know she was feeling like she'd been run over by a bull.

His face was grim, mouth set. He didn't get into the truck, though, so it must not be a complete fail.

"What's the verdict?" she asked.

"They have space."

"Oh good."

"But only one room."

Her high hopes for that hot bath bottomed out somewhere in the dust on the soles of her boots. "What does that mean for us then?"

His gray gaze settled on her, and that deep electric tingle took up residence in her belly. How odd to think that she'd only met him in person this morning. A lot had happened in one day, and she felt as if she'd known him months.

"Could mean a couple things. One, you take the room and I'll sleep in the truck."

She twisted her lips. As much as she wanted to relax alone for the night, she didn't want to think of Aiden out here alone in the uncomfortable truck.

"What's the other option?"

His gaze speared her to the seat. "We share the room."

"Is there only one bed?" she hazarded.

He gave a brief businesslike nod like he was making a deal with the devil. It amused her that he was so rattled by the thought of sharing a room with her.

"Is there a sofa or something one of us can sleep on?"

He lifted a shoulder in a shrug, looking as uncomfortable as a cat in a cattle stampede. "Dunno. We'll find out if we take the room."

"Okay then. Let's go. I'll pay."

"Not necessary. The department puts us up for the nights we're on the road."

"All right." She got out of the truck. Neither of them had luggage and that meant Amaryllis was going to have to wash her underthings in the sink. Wait—scratch that. Where would she hang them to dry if they were sharing a room? She couldn't exactly leave her panties hanging on the shower rod for Aiden to see.

She pushed out a sigh. She'd been in stickier situations in her years but today was up there on her list of the more difficult ones. But she'd live through it, same as she persevered through everything in life.

She wasn't afraid of a grumpy ex-military lawman who needed a shave and had beat up a man who'd made a comment about her ass.

She was more afraid of how her body reacted to him.

* * * * *

When Aiden opened the door of the room, once glance told him it was the worst case. One bed. A pair of wing-back faux leather chairs with a small table between them in one corner. Maybe a child could scoot those chairs together and find a night's sleep on their combined cushions, but not him.

She stepped past him and blew out a breath. "I'll take the floor."

He bit off a groan. The woman was driving him crazy with her need to man up. He had nothing against strong women. In fact, he preferred them to whiny princesses. But did she really believe he'd let a woman sleep on the floor while he sacked out in comfort?

"I'm sorry I didn't think to tell you to bring a bag." Actually, he figured she'd know better than to head out with no essentials. He always kept a backpack with a spare change of clothes, a toothbrush and a razor.

"I carry one in my truck back home. Guess I'm a bit out of my element here." She went over to the window and pushed aside the curtain. He'd never stayed in this particular place but figured the window must face over the back of the B&B and a big deck.

The days were long at this time of year, but the sun was setting and shadows laying across the land. She turned from the window and met his stare.

Her arms were folded over her sumptuous breasts, and he wondered what the hell she wore to bed. She didn't look like a woman who'd don a nightgown but probably fell into bed in much less.

Great. Now his cock was stirring again. Just what he needed — for her to wake up in the night to spot his dick tenting the covers.

"Should be extra blankets in the closet. Pillows too." He tipped his head toward the closet he spoke of.

She dropped her arms to her sides, looking way more defeated than any woman who'd ever been alone with him in a bedroom. Damn if that didn't irritate the hell out of him.

"Why don't you take a turn at the bathroom first. I want to write some things down."

"Then I'll stay and help you."

"You gonna hold the pen with me?" He gave her a crooked smile.

She blinked at him and then stuttered, "No. I just thought —"

"I know what you thought. Sorry for the teasin'. All right then. Let's write out what we learned today and then create a plan for tomorrow and beyond." He took a chair in the corner and drew out his notebook.

Amaryllis hesitantly seated herself next to him. He could tell by her pose that her muscles were sore. She held her shoulders stiffly and once in a while reached up to massage her neck. His guess was that guy had hit her hard, and being crushed under him on the solid earth hadn't done her body any favors.

Aiden threw a look at the bed, feet away. It was soft, piled with country quilts and fat pillows. Plenty of comfort for rollin' around.

His cock throbbed and for a second, he couldn't focus on the notebook page in front of him.

"9:45," Amaryllis said.

He glanced at her. "What?"

"The time when that happened. 9:45. When we checked out the shed."

His mind had blanked, and all he could think about was giving Amaryllis a nine minute, forty-five second orgasm.

He wrote the detail.

"At eleven you were eating your second pancake. Make note of that." Her tone was completely serious as she gestured to the page.

He issued a low growl. "You might think it's fine to keep track of everything in your head." He tapped his temple the way she had when he'd asked how she remembered details. "But some of us do it this way."

Her brown eyes twinkled with a smile long before her lips quirked upward. His breath punched out of his lungs. Seeing Amaryllis smile, in all her disheveled beauty, only made him want to pick her up and taste her sweet lips.

Right before he tore off her clothes and taught her how good it felt to let go, to give up some of her stronghold on her control and allow him to make the decisions for her.

Like how many times she came. And how far to spread her thighs.

"I'll finish up here. Why don't you have a shower?" he asked.

"Um. Do you think they have an extra toothbrush at the front desk?"

"You may find a toothbrush in one of the drawers under the kitchen sink."

She gave a wry smile. "Wonder if they have a T-shirt for me to sleep in too?"

His cock hardened to full length in one breathy word. T-shirt. Or maybe the word was sleep. Either way, all he could see now was Amaryllis, strawberry-blonde hair tousled, wearing a loose T-shirt with her long legs bare.

And him gliding his hand underneath to find her pussy, hot and wet and begging for a good tonguing. Then a hard fucking.

He grunted to cover his arousal and got up. "That I can help with. I've got a couple in my backpack." He crossed the room to get it. After fumbling with the zipper—his hands were shaking, for God's sake—he pulled out a well-worn T-shirt.

He turned to see her staring at him. A knife of want sliced open an even bigger hole inside him.

He tossed her the shirt and she caught it one-handed. "Thanks." She held it up to read the logo.

"Eagle Crest Ranch." The eagle logo stretched under the arching name of the place he, Judd and Wes had run like wild Indians. They still did.

Amaryllis's warm brown gaze heated him in another way. Fuck—was there a connection between them now? He knew he shouldn't have punched that guy for commenting on her ass. The action had linked his brain in a way he didn't want.

"Is this your ranch you talked about?"

He gave a nod. Trying like hell not to envision her wearing that shirt. Or how horny he'd be next time he wore it, knowing her silky skin had touched the fibers.

"Grew up there. We meet every few weeks if we can get away."

"Where is the ranch located?"

"Sweetwater County."

She tilted her head as if conjuring a mental map of Wyoming. "An hour away?"

"From here, yeah."

She nodded and crumpled the T-shirt against her chest. He never wanted to be a T-shirt so bad in his damn life.

"Guess I'll grab that shower."

"Okay." He shouldn't watch her walk in and close the door. Should not think of her stripping out of her skinny jeans and unbuttoning her top.

To distract himself from the sound of the running water and images of warm spray over Amaryllis's pale skin, he wrote out more notes. He flipped on the TV and then turned it off again. He stared out the window at the deck below. The owner had turned on a set of string lights that ran the perimeter of the deck, making it a magical space. Fireflies twinkled along with them.

Dang, why was he thinking about shit like this?

Because he wanted to take Amaryllis down there and share a beer with her.

A faint *crack* of the bathroom door opening sounded, and he whirled from the window. Steam rolled out and she emerged. Long hair, wet and dangling over her shoulder to dampen the Eagle Crest T-shirt.

He dropped his gaze to her breasts, free and ripe, unhindered by a bra. Fucking hell.

His pulse thundered in his ears.

Dipping his gaze lower, he skimmed over the hem that hung mid-thigh on her. Above that was sweet, sweet heaven. And below, curvy thighs tapered down to muscled calves and dainty ankles.

She made a noise and he snapped his gaze back to hers. She had her clothes bundled in a neat stack, and he wondered if he'd find her panties in there.

Need gathered inside him like a storm, clouds banking for a huge explosion of thunder and lightning.

"Your turn." Her voice was throaty.

He nodded and went to gather his backpack. She hotfooted it to the bed and stripped back the covers. The last glimpse of her before he closed the bathroom door was her backside, the hem riding higher on her thighs as she bent to arrange the sheets.

* * * * *

This was the worst idea Amaryllis had ever gone along with. She should have slept in the bed of Aiden's truck. Anything had to be better than this awkwardness of sharing a room with a man she was far too attracted to.

And, if the smolder in his gaze was anything to go by, he was too.

She was wearing his damn T-shirt, for Chrissakes. It held a piney scent just like the owner, and she'd nearly chickened out about putting it on. But her own top wasn't long enough and no way was she wearing constricting skinny jeans to bed.

Her panties had presented another problem. She couldn't wash them out and wearing them again after getting a shower didn't feel right. In the end, she'd left them off. But that was a huge mistake too, because her inner thighs were damp with need.

Plus, she worried if he could see through the thin fabric and detect she wasn't wearing any underwear.

She eyed the bed. She could be primly snuggled beneath the covers when he came out of the bathroom. Her mind fogged. What did he wear to bed?

With a sigh, she turned from the bed and walked to the closet. She gathered the bedding folded there and carried it to the floor in front of the window. She spread out two quilts on the floor for padding and fluffed the pillows before laying them down. Finally, she unfurled a quilt over the whole thing and folded it neatly for him to slide under.

She looked between his bed and hers. No denying she felt bad. Would it be so awful to share the bed? He wouldn't take up much space.

Who was she kidding? He'd eat up every inch of the bed, leaving her clinging to the edge. Maybe she should offer at least.

The door opened. Steam flooded out. Aiden's shower had to go down in the record books as the quickest ever. The man's bathing habits were as no-nonsense as the rest of him.

"Looks inviting," he drawled from the doorway.

She spun. Did he mean... *her*? No, he had to be talking about the bed on the floor.

She lifted a shoulder in a shrug. "I hope it's okay. I'm really sorry."

"Well, I was gonna say you should have called ahead and gotten us two rooms. But I didn't want to mention it." His grin accompanied his sarcastic words.

"What would we have done if this place didn't have a room open?"

"Driven on. I got a few good hours left in me."

She looked closely at his face. Lined with fatigue and sporting half-moons under each eye. He'd been running on no sleep for almost two days. How was the man even standing?

That was when she noticed his arms. In a short-sleeved T-shirt, the inky lines of tattoos roped around each bicep and disappeared upward out of sight.

Her breathing picked up. What were the tattoos? She never would have suspected he sported those under his clothes. He seemed so straight-laced, old-fashioned almost. But he *had* been in the military, and it was commonplace for men who served to get tattooed.

She swallowed, mouth suddenly dry.

"Well, you must be tired."

"You too."

She rubbed at her neck. The cords were tense, bulging with the strain her neck had taken earlier.

Aiden took a step in her direction, drawing attention to his fresh pair of jeans. Perfectly worn, molded to his body as if made for him. "Your neck hurts. Sit down on the bed."

His commanding tone shouldn't send pangs of sensation between her thighs. Her pussy grew wetter.

She looked into his eyes.

"Sit," he said more gently, softly.

She moved to the bed and perched on the corner. He came to stand in front of her, big body crowded so close that heat wafted off his body and scorched through the thin shirt she wore. She kept her knees together, though it would be easier for him to stand between her legs.

He reached out and brushed her damp hair over her shoulder. When his warm, rough fingers enveloped her sore muscle, she moaned in pure delight.

Aiden went still but she swore a shudder ripped through him. Was he feeling the same attraction and unadulterated desires she was?

This was her work colleague, her partner. They were tossed together to solve the crimes in the area. After she'd done that, she'd be on her way back to Texas and hopefully to her dream of a small farm. Which reminded her — she needed to text her brothers and let them know she'd made it fine.

The small circles Aiden traced on her neck with his fingers made thoughts of her brothers fly out her ears. She angled her head to give him better access. He moved up and down the column of her throat, dipping his fingers into the hollow of her shoulder.

She groaned.

"That's sore too?"

She breathed out. "Yes."

"Relax. Let me do this for you."

She wanted to look up at his face but was afraid she'd see the want burning in his eyes. If she saw it, she didn't know if she'd deny him.

It would be so easy to let him tumble her into the sheets, open her thighs and invite him in.

Enough. I have to stop this.

"That's good. I'm better now. Thank you." Her words came out choppy, no gratitude in her tone.

He dropped his hands immediately and stepped back. She tested her neck by looking up at him. His chest heaved, and his square jaw set so hard it looked capable of flaying open an enemy.

"Glad it helped. I'll hit the floor now."

"Roshannon—" She broke off before the words escaped to ask him to sleep there next to her where it was more comfortable.

He arched a brow but said nothing.

"Good day on the job today. Goodnight."

A spark died down in his gray eyes but they appeared even stormier than before. "Night." He crossed the room to the pallet on the floor, shutting off lights on the way.

Had she really just praised him for a good day on the job? After their hours together, she felt there was more between them. A friendship almost, though he didn't agree with her methods.

Aiden Roshannon was a hard man with a set of ironclad rules. She'd obviously broken most of them today. With a smile as she crawled under the covers, she realized tomorrow she might do even better at bucking his system.

As his snore hit her almost immediately, she lay staring into the darkness, her mind going a mile a minute and her body still tingling from his touch that had gone way beyond her neck.

* * * * *

Aiden started awake, eyes wide, staring into the blackness. His heart raced, pounding against his chest wall painfully as the remnants of his dream faded from his consciousness.

The village spread out below, tiny and vulnerable. Packed with innocent people. And one big building, the rooms filled with enemies.

One choice. One blast.

The order he'd refused to take. The one that had gotten him hauled home to the States and questioned for hours until he'd felt he'd crack under the pressure.

I couldn't follow orders, sir. I couldn't kill innocent people.

That building was full of five of the most wanted criminals on our list. They've kidnapped and tortured US citizens, Roshannon. What don't you understand about that?

But the houses around that building would have been blown off the map in the blast. I couldn't do it, sir.

And on and on.

He stood, the covers puddling on the floor. Disoriented, he turned in the dark toward the only light source—moonlight streaming in from the curtain nearby.

Everything flooded back to him—the B&B. What the hell was it called? His mind was still back in fucking Iraq. He concentrated and conjured a name.

Silverblossom. The name of the B&B where he and Amaryllis had stopped for the night.

Amaryllis.

He sought out the chairs in the corner and made his way to one. It faced the bed and by now his eyes had adjusted to the darkness. He sank into one and dropped his head into his hands, breathing evenly to dispel the anxiety inside him. That sensation of his skin bursting open to let the bad stuff escape wouldn't leave him for a long time, he knew. He'd been dealing with it for a year now.

The outline of Amaryllis on the bed drew his gaze. He made out a shoulder, a soft hip rising up under the quilt. He wanted to turn on the light and see her hair scattered across the pillow, her face in repose.

125

A beautiful woman, so close. Invitingly close. He could crawl into bed with her and gain the comfort he needed.

Fuck that—he was a goddamn Marine with years of combat in his past. He didn't need comfort from anybody.

Except she looked so good lying there. He could just put his arms around her, draw her body back against his.

He scrubbed his hands over his face and worked on his oxygen consumption. Too much and he'd get that dizzy, spinning feeling. If he held his breath, he only felt worse.

Sweat trickled down his bare spine, all the way to his jeans.

Five feet away, Amaryllis was wearing his T-shirt.

He must have made a noise, because she sat up suddenly. Through the darkness, they stared at each other.

"Roshannon?"

"Yeah. It's okay. Go back to sleep." His voice was gruff.

The covers rustled and he realized she was getting out of bed. He tensed. If she came close enough wearing only his T-shirt, he couldn't account for his actions. The dream, his hungers and Amaryllis were all mixed up in his head. A cocktail for disaster.

Her footstep on the carpet made his fucking skin prickle. Behind his fly, his cock stirred. Fuck, he wanted her to beg for him, to hear her cries of pleasure-pain and give him all the control inside this bedroom that he craved.

She stepped up to him. He locked his hands on the armrests of the chair and sat all the way back. "Go back to bed, Amaryllis."

"What's going on? You don't sound okay."

Because I'm not. I want to fuck you so hard that you'll never be fit for another man the rest of your life.

She stood inches away, long hair floating around her torso in a riot of waves. A bead of moonlight on her bare thighs.

She reached out and skimmed a touch over each of his biceps. He jerked.

"Your tattoos… All day, I never knew they were there."

"Well, now you do." *And if you don't get your hands off me, you'll be sorry. We'll both be sorry, woman.*

"Can I turn on the light?"

"No," he said at once. If he got one clear look into her eyes, he'd be a goner. He'd pick her up, toss her on the bed and spear her with his cock. Fucking away all the pain and hunger burning inside him.

But she wouldn't like him in the morning. Hell, she didn't like him now.

And he'd hate himself.

She continued to stand there, touching him. He swallowed hard, his throat dry and itchy.

"We'll catch the rustlers, Roshannon."

A noise broke from him. Christ, she thought he was sitting up worrying about the job. But now that she'd mentioned it, his mind hit the ground running, covering the ground of the case they'd been following the previous day and what might come on day two of the auction.

Amaryllis stroked her fingers over his arms, shooting sparks of liquid desire through his entire body. He felt like he'd been dunked in an electrified pool of water, helpless and sinking by the minute.

She moved her hands up to his shoulders, rock-hard with tension. She kneaded the muscles.

He shrugged her off. "Stop."

"Sometimes I hate traveling. Waking up in a strange room, wondering where the hell I am and what I'm supposed to be doing." Her whispered admission slammed him. "Do you ever feel that way?"

"Fuck, woman. You need to go back to bed."

She didn't move. Contrary woman that she was. Spirited, stubborn. And everything he fucking wanted, if he was honest with himself.

One day and he wanted her. He'd met her face-to-face less than twenty-four fucking hours ago, and he was ready to claim her in ways that neither of them could never go back on.

"Aiden..."

The sound of his name on her lips did him in. He caught her by the hips and jerked her down on his lap. Her ass fit his body perfectly, cradling his cock, now hard at the first contact.

She made a noise of surprise, and he found the point of her chin in the darkness. Pinching it lightly, he tipped her head up to meet his gaze. Her face was mostly in shadow, her eyes shiny.

"I can't put my hands on you, Amaryllis."

"Then why are you?" Her tone held that note of sass that had driven him nuts half the day. Now he understood why. It was fucking foreplay to him. She mouthed off, and he wanted to shut her up with long, deep kisses.

"Why are you touching me, Aiden?"

"Stop asking questions I can't answer."

"I think you can answer."

"Because I'm selfish."

"I don't think that's true." She stared deep into his eyes, leaning nearer by the fucking second. He felt the heat of her breath on his jaw. All he had to do was move half an inch and he'd have her lips under his.

Because until this afternoon when I punched that man for commenting on your ass, I didn't know what I needed in my life to make me feel like a man again.

He'd spent a year trying to make his job with the sheriff's office into his whole life the way the military had been. He was dedicated to the ranchers, would do anything for them. All this time, he'd smoldered with anger—at the command he'd been given, at himself for not being the Marine he should have been. If he'd taken action, five less monsters would be walking the earth right now.

But he'd refused the order and the men had fled the bunker through underground tunnels before Aiden's commanding officer realized he wasn't going to make the move.

That time of his life had sucked, and he'd spent the past year feeling lost.

Amaryllis had walked into his life and in less than twenty-four fucking hours, he knew exactly what his purpose on this planet was.

To pick her up and seat her on his face, make her scream for him.

He moved his hand to her lower back, feeling the slipperiness of her skin under the cotton of his T-shirt.

"Aiden."

"Time like this, I wish you'd call me Roshannon." At least then he could take an order to back off, let her go.

She issued a choppy breath. Hell, she still smelled like toothpaste.

"Fine. Roshannon, why do I want you to kiss me?"

"Goddammit, Amaryllis. Why do I want to?" He cupped the back of her head, sinking his fingers deep into her hair, and claimed her mouth.

The first crush of her lips under his sent him whirling. Yet he had complete control. He pulled her closer, molding her to fit his form as he probed the seam of her lips with his tongue.

On a whimper, she opened for him, and he plunged deep inside. One pass, two. His fucking cock was hard steel digging into her backside. She clutched his biceps, fingers over his semper fi tattoo that said Saint Michael Protect Us. And the American flag rippling on his left arm, surrounded by stars, one for every friend he'd lost.

He nibbled at her lower lip, pulling a harsh cry from her. More of that and he wouldn't stop until every hunger inside him was sated. She dug her blunt nails into his skin and raked them back to his shoulders.

The searing sensation of her scoring him had him locked and loaded. He gripped her by the hip and wrapped her hair around his fist simultaneously. Levering her down into his cock as he tugged her strawberry-blonde locks and ravished her mouth.

She scrabbled at his shoulders, matching his kisses stroke for stroke.

He broke the kiss and yanked her head back, biting into her throat as he worked his hand up to cup her breast.

She jolted.

"Aiden, stop."

Ice water struck him in the face, and he jerked his hands from her. She didn't move off his lap.

"I'm sorry." His voice sounded like tearing cloth.

"I-I did it too. Got carried away."

Yeah, but he'd scared her. When he'd gotten rough with her, she'd ended the play. She'd never accept what he was, even if she knew more.

"Go back to bed, Amaryllis. We have to get up early." Though he'd never sleep now, and she probably wouldn't either. She'd lie in bed and he'd toss and turn on the hard floor, wanting her with everything in him.

He pushed out a breath and when she didn't get off his lap, he gave her a little push onto her feet.

She stood there, arms wrapped around herself, which only made his T-shirt ride up almost to her crotch.

He swore from the heat he'd felt through his jeans that she wasn't wearing panties. But he couldn't find out.

"I'm sorry for touching you," he said.

"I… don't do this. I wanted you to know. Not ever."

Meaning what? She didn't sit on the laps of men she'd known less than a full day? Or didn't accept the womanly needs that had obviously pounded through her only seconds before?

He gave a harsh nod. "All right."

She stood there for another long heartbeat. He clamped his jaw so tight that his molars met with a *clack.*

Then she turned and moved back to the bed, her feet soundless. She crawled under the covers and turned her back to him.

He sat there longer until he thought he heard Amaryllis' deep breathing of sleep. Then

he lay down on the floor and tried to find some
damn peace.

Chapter Seven

Neither of them mentioned the big, horny elephant in the room the next morning or all through breakfast. They rode to the auction in silence and when they got there, Amaryllis took an opportunity to break away from Roshannon.

She had no idea what to do about the kiss they'd shared — or the fact that she wanted more. So she threw herself into work.

While inspecting the cattle, she kept an eye out for anything suspicious, but this day of the auction seemed to be on the up-and-up. She chatted with people and got a few names of men she wanted to investigate.

The auctioneer was going full-force, his garbled words tripping over each other as he worked the prices up. On day two of wearing the same outfit, Amaryllis was ready to get home. But she hadn't seen Roshannon in the past two hours to find out when he planned to leave.

She sat back in the stands while the bidding continued around her and pulled out her phone. JD had texted more about the small farm. Said he knew a friend who could talk to her more about the topic when she was ready.

She blinked at the words on her screen. Right now, up here in Wyoming, owning a farm had been far from her mind. When she thought of it now, she wondered if she really wanted to settle down and farm a piece of land. It wasn't the hard work she was afraid of. It was just…

She loved the thrill that being a Ranger offered. Working with the ranchers, helping them through more than investigating crimes against them. It was times she assisted with brush fires and rounding up cattle from flooded conditions. There was always something to keep her on her toes.

She wasn't sure if hunting down the best heirloom melon seeds for her farm would offer the same kick.

After exchanging a few texts with JD, she flipped through some selfies he'd sent her on Snapchat.

A grunt sounded behind her. She glanced over her shoulder to see Aiden sitting there, making no pretenses about spying on her phone activity.

"Thought you were on the job," he said in an even tone that was much too nonchalant to be real.

She shut her lips tight to keep from spewing harsh replies. She had to ride back to Crossroads with him, and things were tense enough.

With a sigh, she smoothed her hair over her shoulder. It was frizzy today, and no wonder. Between the cheap B&B's shampoo and terrible sleep she'd gotten, she'd woke up looking like the Mad Hatter. Not to mention she didn't have a hairbrush and she'd had to finger-comb the tangles out.

She also smelled like Aiden. That masculine scent clung to her, and she could still feel the rough burn of his beard against her cheeks when he'd kissed her.

She squirmed on the hard, wooden bench and flipped open Snapchat again to keep from engaging in an argument with Roshannon. JD had sent her another snap, this one of the lower half of his face and a big fat donut hanging from his mouth.

Aiden gave another grunt. "Your boyfriend?"

She stilled. So that was it. He was goading her because he was jealous.

At the same time, it pissed her off that he'd believe she had a boyfriend and had still sat on his lap kissing him.

She twisted to pierce him in her stare. And nearly gasped at how much his beard had grown in since she'd seen him a few hours ago. Almost black, thick—and dangerous to her female sensibilities.

"You didn't bother asking me if I had a boyfriend last night."

His eyes sparked. "You didn't mention it when you snuggled into my lap."

She threw a look at the men sitting around them, but nobody seemed to be paying attention to them, too focused on the sale of a pair of good workhorses.

"You *pulled me down* there, Roshannon."

He narrowed his gaze but said nothing.

She whirled to face forward again but a second later stood and started excusing herself to the men seated around her as she made her way toward the exit. She didn't make it two steps into the dreary outdoors when fingers bit into her elbow.

Aiden spun her to face him and dragged her to a stop at the same time. They faced off, her breath heaving with the need to scream, stomp her feet—and go on tiptoe and kiss the hell out of him.

His eyes were serious, the same color as the leaden sky above. "Look, I'm sorry. We have a lot of work to do together, and we shouldn't let this affect that."

"Exactly. Let's pretend it never happened." *That you woke up things inside me that I don't want to forget.*

He released her arm and tugged his hat lower over his eyes. "I agree. Let's get on home. There's nothing more to learn here."

The ride was made in relative silence, and by the time he pulled into the station, Amaryllis was done with being in his presence. She needed some breathing room and time to think about how she was going to deal with the needs he'd awakened inside her.

She got out of the truck and slammed the door. "See you later." Without a backward glance, she went to her silly little rental car and climbed behind the wheel.

He peeled out, the truck tires grinding on the gravel as he gunned it out of the parking lot. She shook her head and forced herself to drive at a normal pace and not race after him like a maniac, though she wanted to.

Mind reeling through several ways to make him see he was acting like an immature ass, she drove to the B&B where the sheriff's office had set her up. The place was much different from the one she'd stayed at with Aiden, and she was relieved to walk into a space she didn't have to share with the man.

Her own bed, without worrying about how uncomfortable he must be on the floor. Not to mention the midnight kiss they'd shared.

She stripped off her clothes and took a hot shower. But the water was only making her think of warm parts of her body. Between her thighs, her body was ten degrees hotter. And she ached.

She hadn't brought any battery-operated toys from home, and now she regretted the decision. She needed release now.

She leaned against the shower wall, letting the spray wash over her as she slipped her fingers over her pussy. Fuck, she was already creamy with desire. She trapped her clit under two fingers and massaged. Sensation hit full-force, weakening her knees. She used the wall for support as she fingered herself into a frenzy. Her breaths came in hitching gulps, and she swore she felt the tugging on her scalp as Aiden had tugged the strands while plundering her mouth.

She circled her clit and inserted one finger into her pussy. Two pumps and she was coming in long, gasping waves. Juices flooded her fingers, and sharp cries left her lips.

When the final pulsation left her, she sank down the shower wall and closed her eyes. The man was going to kill her.

Aiden sprawled on his bed, naked and facedown. His cock harder than the stone face of Obsidian Cliff. His body warred, tearing him in two directions.

He needed sleep—badly. His nerves were jumping and if he got a call right now, he wasn't sure he had the energy to get up and go.

And second, he needed release. His balls were splitting, throbbing in a way that warned him that he needed to come—soon. If he didn't slake his lust, there was no telling what he might do.

Last time he'd gotten this horny, he'd ended up fucking a woman right in front of his cousin's eyes. Of course, after he'd rolled away from her, Wes had taken his place. But Aiden didn't want to share Amaryllis.

Wait — who's talking about Amaryllis?

Who was he kidding? She was the reason he was lying here ready to rut like a bull. But he'd never share her with any man, because she was going to be his and his alone.

He rolled onto his back and cradled his balls in one hand while wrapping his other fist around his length. He squeezed his shaft and let out a groan. Looking down at himself, he found the head of his cock was swollen, purple. The slit glistening with pre-cum.

Amaryllis had done this to him, and he was going to use her until he was satisfied or passed out. Whichever came first.

He rolled his cock through his fist. Arching in pleasure as sensation hit. His mind traveled back to having Amaryllis in his lap with only a thin bit of cotton between him and her sweet pussy. Her mouth open wide to accept his kisses. Then carrying her to the bed and pinning her to the mattress. Making her beg him to suck her nipples, eat her pussy.

Groaning loudly, he pumped his cock harder. Faster. When he claimed her, she'd feel every inch of him deep inside her, and there wouldn't be anyone else.

Then he'd tell her when she could come for him and if she didn't obey, he'd start all over from the top, this time tying her to the bed. Kissing and biting every inch of her. Spanking her round ass and finally gliding into her tight pussy—

He came in a rush. Hot semen spilled over his knuckles and a low roar vibrated the mattress. Images of ropes knotted up and down Amaryllis' pale body flashed behind his eyes as the final spurts left him.

Goddammit, what was he going to do with this wanting now that it was unloosed again?

He couldn't direct it toward her. She was probably frightened enough by him. Besides, she had a boyfriend.

Then why was his mind screaming at him to get up and go to her? Barge into her room at the Crossroads Inn and tell her that they might have only known each other for a short time, but there was unfinished business between them.

Damn, he needed to talk to someone. It was time they all went home to Eagle Crest.

* * * * *

"How's things working out with Amaryllis?" Sheriff Latchaw eyed Aiden from the doorway.

Aiden set his jaw as he met Latchaw's gaze. He could tell the sheriff that she wasn't answering his calls and when he'd swung by the Crossroads Inn, her rental car was gone. Either she was working solo today or she'd quit the job altogether and run scared.

"You're a tough one to work with, Roshannon. You're used to sharing your thoughts with very few people, but you're going to have to find a way to include Amaryllis in this case."

"I would if I could find her," he bit off. Sick and tired of hearing how he was a hard man to work with, talk to, be around. If people didn't like him, they could just keep their fucking distances. Amaryllis included.

Only he didn't want her to. Which almost had *him* running scared.

"What do you mean you can't find her?" Latchaw's tone didn't leave room for wishy-washy answers.

He opened his mouth to speak when a loud rumble of engine outside made him and Latchaw turn to the window. Through the slats of blinds, they saw a huge diesel 4x4 truck pulling into the parking lot.

The red truck swung wide to park in a spot next to Aiden's truck, dwarfing it. Then the door opened and a woman jumped what had to be three feet to the ground.

Latchaw burst out laughing. "Think I found your partner."

"Where the hell'd she even find a truck like that?" Their small town didn't boast car rental places, and nobody had trucks like that—they were too impractical in these parts.

"I think she's trying to show you who's got the bigger set of balls." Latchaw brought his hand down on Aiden's shoulder. "Good luck, Roshannon."

Aiden pushed out a breath through his nostrils and watched Amaryllis approach the office. And she was fucking beautiful.

Wearing dark jeans and cowgirl boots, a simple white T-shirt that skimmed her breasts, and sunglasses. Her hair loose underneath her cowgirl hat.

Without realizing it, he'd stood and was prying apart the blinds to see more of her.

"She's fucking hot, isn't she?" Hoyt's observation made Aiden spin, hands fisted at his sides.

He hadn't made up his mind yet if he was pursuing Amaryllis and this dark need she created in him. But Hoyt sure as fuck wasn't.

The front door slammed and he knew she was in the building. "Hello, Diana," she called out to the secretary.

"Hi, Ms. Long. You're looking bright-eyed today."

"I am. Where's Latchaw?"

"In his office, far as I know."

Aiden shoved Hoyt out of the way to get out his office door. Why was she asking for Latchaw and not him?

He pushed into the hall in time to see her breeze past, hair bouncing on her spine, and her bootheels ringing on the old linoleum tile. She threw him a smile and kept on going.

145

A growl rose in his throat. What was she playing at?

"Nice truck, Amaryllis," Latchaw said by way of greeting.

Aiden walked into his office behind Amaryllis without invitation.

"I found something, sir. I need a warrant."

Aiden felt his blood pressure jack up ten points. His ears burned. "You were on the job this morning without me?"

She ignored his question and planted a hand on Latchaw's desk to lean over and speak to the sheriff, excluding Aiden. "That neighbor of Owens' we talked to yesterday…"

"You went over there again? So help me, woman," Aiden cut her off.

"Excuse me, but my momma taught me that interrupting's rude. Didn't yours?"

Latchaw smiled and looked between the two.

"The neighbor had a stack of papers on the table and one of the names caught my eye."

Aiden stilled. Heart thumping with fury. "What the hell are you talking about?" And why hadn't she mentioned it to him?

She didn't even look his way let alone answer him. "I did some digging on the guy we apprehended two days ago at auction. And a name kept coming up in association with him."

Latchaw sat forward. Aiden wanted to punch something. Why hadn't he discovered any of this information? It was his fucking case, his fucking county. Hell, his state. Amaryllis was hijacking everything.

"Give me the name." Latchaw drew a sheet of paper toward him.

"Fitz. Michael J Fitz. From Rock Springs."

Aiden searched his mind for memory of that name. Nothing.

"Do you have any reason to issue a warrant, Amaryllis? I can't just send you off on a wild lead."

She looked at Aiden and gave a single nod. "I have record that he just sold nine hundred pounds of beef to a butcher in Rock Springs for pennies on the dollar. When I spoke to the butcher, he told me Fitz said he had to unload it quick, needed the freezer space."

Latchaw nodded, the grin back on his face. "That's a credible lead."

"And turns out he rents an old building outside of Crossroads."

Aiden narrowed his eyes. "Which one is that?"

"The grocery store. Willy's. My guess is there's a big walk-in freezer and plenty of coolers to store trafficked beef. I need a warrant to search the place."

"You got it, little lady. I'll got the magistrate on it. Consider it done." Latchaw smiled.

She dropped Aiden a sweet smile. "Comin' with me, Roshannon? I'll drive."

Chapter Eight

Aiden's low growl seemed to vibrate all the way down Amaryllis's spine. Somehow she kept walking, each long stride across the parking lot a step toward her goal. She had to keep her eyes on the prize, and right now, it was finding the people involved in committing these crimes.

She didn't have time for hot cowboy lawmen with hidden tattoos or lips that could seduce the Virgin Mary.

His stomps crunched the gravel parking area like he was determined to smash the rock to dust. "What do you think you're doing, investigating without me?"

She kept walking. "Just found out. I don't for a minute believe if you'd gotten a taste of this that you wouldn't have investigated right away, too."

"You should have called. Texted. Dropped by my place. I'm sure you know where I live."

She did. Crossroads was small and people knew everything. She'd driven by his place, wondering at how a man like Aiden Roshannon was content with the small rental house and postage stamp-sized yard. He seemed like a man who needed to roam.

Reaching the truck, she clicked the key fob to unlock the doors. She had to admit, the monster truck was more perfect than she'd hoped for in a rental. When she'd called ahead for a vehicle and told the business to provide her with the biggest pickup they could wrangle up, she'd never pictured this.

She reached up for the door handle. Thank God it had running boards, but she still had to lift her leg high to reach it.

"Jesus, woman. You're a piece of work." She knew Aiden was shaking his head even if she didn't see it. "Let me drive."

"No way, Roshannon." She opened the door and launched inside. He could come with her or drive himself. Either way, she was getting to the abandoned grocery store in this beauty.

A heartbeat later, he whipped open the passenger door and landed in the seat, glare hot, fists clenched on his knees.

She smiled at him. "You know what they say about girls and their trucks." She looked at lifted trucks the way men looked at her ass.

"Uh-huh. Diesel makes her clothes fall off."

She gulped midway through starting the engine. How the hell was she supposed to come back from that comment when her mind was completely blank? Wiped clean by his words and images of them naked in the monster truck bed?

He reached out and tapped on her lower jaw, snapping it shut. With a huff of irritation, she faced forward and drove out of the lot. Careful not to lay on the gas and spray gravel over the vehicles there. Aiden's she wasn't so concerned about, but she didn't want to do damage to the sheriff's or deputies'.

"Turn right," he ordered.

"I know, Roshannon. Spent half the night figuring out most of the roads around here." She didn't tell him it was because she couldn't sleep. Or how her body had been so keyed up that she'd pleasured herself several times.

She kept her gaze on the highway and navigating the twisty roads around the base of the mountain range.

"You didn't tell me you looked into Fitz."

She threw him a look. "Anybody who knows crime would."

"We had Latchaw running the information."

"Sometimes you gotta do things differently."

"Outside the law you mean."

"Maybe."

"How'd you do it? Did you call Judd?"

She stumbled over that name. "Your twin?"

He was fuming so bad she swore steam was raising off his skull underneath his hat. "The very same."

"No. I have strings I can pull. I made a call to a bounty hunter I know."

At that, he gripped the console so hard she thought he might leave finger dents. "Wes?"

She racked her brain for that name, and it came to her after a couple seconds. "Not your cousin. I've got a friend who works the entire West, from north to south. He only needs a name most of the time, because he has access to a massive data base."

"I can't believe you, Amaryllis."

He didn't sound too happy about her making the discovery without him. Then again, Roshannon didn't seem like a happy man in general.

"What's your middle name?"

It was his turn to be caught off-guard. "What?"

"What's your middle name?"

"Why?"

152

"I thought it might be Grumpy."

"You haven't seen anything yet." His tone was a low oath.

He didn't tell her his middle name, and she thought pressuring him might make his hat combust. She settled against the leather seat and drove.

The small suburb of Crossroads was basically a ghost town, stamped on the map with disappearing ink. She looked at the one main street. A few houses still had flags out front, waving in the mountain breeze. But nobody was around.

"What happened to this place?" she asked.

"You mean you didn't already ask around and find out?"

"Roshannon," she warned.

"Fine. Classic tale of a bigger road going in. Easier to drive, especially in winters. People stopped coming this way and the few stores went out of business, which meant people had no conveniences and they moved away."

"It's a pretty place. For a ghost town."

"I always liked it. Store's on the left if you don't know."

She didn't and passed it. Aiden snorted but said nothing as she backed up and parked in the lot. The pavement had a network of cracks with weeds growing in them.

Aiden placed a hand on the door handle. "So when's the owner meeting us to let us in the building?"

He wasn't going to like this part.

"He's not." She jumped out of the truck before she could hear his response. But as soon as her boots were on the ground, he came around the vehicle, cussing.

"What the fuck do you mean he's not coming to let us in? We have a warrant but that doesn't mean breaking and entering."

"Who said anything about that?" She only took a step toward the small hometown-style grocery store when Aiden wrapped his fingers around her elbow.

She stopped at the warmth seeping into her skin. And how it reminded her of being in his lap, his hands on her body making her burn hotter as he kissed her.

No way was she going to look at him. She didn't want to see what was in his eyes, what might have been between them that night in the B&B.

He hovered close. If she tipped her head back, their hats would brush. She focused on the buttons of his chambray shirt. Earlier, she'd noticed how the faded blue made his gray eyes stand out like thunderclouds, but she couldn't look at them now.

"Amaryllis, we are not entering this building without the owner letting us in." His tone brooked no argument.

"We won't need to."

"What the hell are you talkin' about, woman?"

"You know, some ladies would be offended at being called woman. You're lucky I'm not one of them."

He made a sound that was almost a chuckle. Liquid heat pooled low in her belly. A spark of arousal made her pussy clench.

"We're just going to walk around the perimeter first."

He released her arm, and she felt cold air claim the spot where his fingers had been. "Let's go."

The building was shut tight, the front door sprouting rust in spots but securely bolted. The big glass windows were lined with butcher paper that said OUT OF BUSINESS. They walked around to the side and found a door where employees might have come out to have smoke breaks. A few old cigarette butts still littered the parking lot.

Aiden knocked on the door.

Amaryllis almost laughed out loud but bit it off. This man was a stickler for the rules and a martyr of politeness. She doubted he'd fart in his own house without asking his cat if it was okay first.

If he had a cat.

He walked ahead of her, and it was impossible not to admire the man's broad shoulders and torso that tapered to his waist. Worn jeans barely clung to his hips and the denim stretched across his hard thighs with each step he took.

If he wasn't her partner, she'd think he was hot.

Hell, who was she kidding? She thought so now.

And he was a damn fine kisser.

Stop it, Amaryllis.

"You have a girlfriend, Roshannon?"

He skidded to a stop and looked around at her. Eyes blazing under the brim of his hat. "What?"

Shit, she shouldn't have let that question slip. Too late to go back now.

"Do you have a girlfriend?"

He gave her that slow once-over that was like sliding an ice cube over her searing hot skin in the heatwave of a Texas summer. Her nipples peaked and her pussy throbbed.

"No, I don't."

"Oh."

"Why do you ask?"

"Just figured we should know each other better. And if you have one, I should meet her. Sometimes women don't like me working with their significant others."

He grunted. Dang, if grunting was a language, he was a freaking master.

They rounded another corner of the building and saw the muddy tire tracks at the same time.

Aiden bent to inspect them more closely. "Someone was off-roading to get this much mud on their tires." He followed the tracks with his gaze out to where the parking lot ended. "I'd say he drove across the fields to this point."

"ATV?" she asked, leaning over.

He nodded and scooped up a crumble of mud. He crushed it into dust in his fingers and let it fall. "Bringing butchered meat in the back door."

"That's my thinking." She walked up to the building and yanked the door. It was locked. But a small line of windows on the side of the building surely were opened for ventilation now and then. One could be accidentally left unlocked.

She started down the line, pushing and pulling. Two wouldn't budge, but the third had a glass pane that rattled in its metal frame.

She threw a look over her shoulder at Aiden.

"Don't you dare, Amaryllis."

"Don't worry, Roshannon. Nothing'll get broken."

* * * * *

How the damn woman knew how to pop a pane of glass out of a window frame without breaking it, he didn't want to know. She probably doubled as a cat burglar when she wasn't out hurling herself at cattle rustlers.

She set aside the glass, leaning it against the building.

"Now what?" He wanted to haul her over, strip her pants down to her ankles and flog her good. Then make her scream with pleasure.

She surveyed the opening she'd made, about chest high on her. "I might need a boost."

"Only boost you're getting from me is when I toss you back into that monster truck o' yours and drive your ass back to Crossroads."

She gave him a shake of her head as if disappointed in him. "Fine, I can shimmy up and in."

"Then what? I can't let you go in there alone. What if Fitz has someone in there?"

He pictured scenario after scenario, each involving gunfire, Amaryllis taken hostage and Aiden going ballistic on this side of the wall trying to get to her.

"I don't think anybody's in here. Sure you won't give me a leg up, Roshannon? Just like you're helping a woman into the saddle. Not that I believe you've ever done that in your life."

He pushed out a forceful breath through his nose. "Fine. Gimme your foot." He crouched and cupped his hands together. She placed a boot in his palms and pushed upward. She caught the window frame with her hands and pulling herself the rest of the way up and through.

The windows were too grubby back here to see through, but he heard her hit the floor.

"You all right?" he called.

"Peachy."

He rolled his eyes. Fuck, she was killing him. Each throb of his heart counted for two subtracted from his life.

He pulled off his hat and scraped his fingers through his hair. He was sweating. She was breaking all the rules and he was standing here watching h—

159

Thoughts breaking off at the sound of a door opening, he turned immediately toward the noise. Prepared to see a gun held to Amaryllis's temple and a crazy fucker with his finger on the trigger.

But she stood there alone, perky breasts riding high and a grin on her beautiful face. "C'mon."

Jesus, he was as nuts as she was. After knowing her a few weeks, he was ready to retire.

Or fuck her the way he needed.

Her curvy backside disappeared into the dark space, and he followed. Inside, it was dim with the only light shining through the bank of windows. Big shapes loomed up, metal containers with wheels used to move slabs of meat and shopping carts in a corner. She bumped into something and he ran into her from behind. His groin crushed against her sweet little ass.

He groaned and reflexively grabbed her by the hips.

He heard the breath trickle from her. "Aiden."

"Just making sure you've got your footing." He didn't let her go. The fucking urge to buck against her ass was tooth-grindingly real.

"I... do," she said on an exhalation.

He released her and clamped his fingers into fists to keep from spinning her into his embrace. Lifting her against a wall and fucking her brains out. Surely there was some rope in here somewhere. Hell, he could fashion one out of old plastic grocery bags.

She took out her phone and used the flashlight app. She waved it around, letting him see the other objects they could trip over.

Distracting himself was key right now. He used his phone's flashlight too and ran it over the floor. Sure enough, blood striped the tile from the door to a meat cooler. He followed it with Amaryllis at his side.

Damn if she wasn't right about Fitz. There was a lot going on with this case, and as much as he didn't want to admit it, Aiden probably wouldn't have gotten this far without her. Having the extra body on the job meant double the effort.

Without a trace of fear in her body, Amaryllis strode up to that walk-in and jerked open the door.

"It's empty," she said in surprise.

"But you can see there's been beef hanging here. Now all we need is a clue as to whose beef it was. Look around for a tag or some hides."

After several minutes of combing the freezer and old butcher shop around it, they were no closer to solving the case.

Aiden did have a huge case of blue-balls, however. Something about being in the dark with Amaryllis made him forget she was a pain in his ass.

He clicked off his light and faced her. Damn if he didn't want to taste her again.

"Why are you looking at me that way?" Her voice trembled.

He took a step toward her.

"Aiden, I don't think—"

"Then don't." He caught her around the middle and yanked her against his body. Her soft breasts molded to his chest, his cock snug against her belly. He cupped her face and claimed what he wanted.

Her lips, for a start.

He'd work on her trust later.

* * * * *

Aiden's mouth blazed across Amaryllis's neck and down to her collarbone. Then he kept on going. Tugging down the material of her T-shirt to spatter kisses over the tops of her breasts.

She clung to him, her breaths harsh in the silent space. She still gripped her phone and had no idea where to put it, but she wanted to slip her arms around his neck and draw him closer.

This attraction needed an outlet, and if it only happened once, then it was probably for the better. At least they would have satisfied their longings.

He took the phone from her hand and set it aside on a metal table in the middle of the room. Then he raised her arms and stripped off her top. Her bra followed, and her skin prickled as air struck her nude flesh. A brief second later his lips landed on her skin, peaking it until she was shivering with need.

"I've been fucking wanting you for days." He took her hand and plastered it over his cock. The bulge made her suck in a sharp breath. He was hard—and big. And she wanted him inside her.

"I thought you didn't like me," she managed to squeak.

"You're a hard woman to get along with. But we do this just fine." He walked his fingers down her spine to her lower back. She wanted to yell at him to stop teasing her already and get on with it. But he seemed to rob her of breath and something inside her wanted to see what he could do without being told.

Aiden's sure touch told her he knew exactly what he wanted from her and how to get it.

He cupped her breasts and raised her nipples to his lips. Soft brushing of lips first and then wet pulls of his mouth that made her knees buckle. He held her up, licking back and forth between her nipples like he was trying to eat two ice cream cones.

Groans emitted from her throat, and she worked at the buttons of his shirt until it hung open. She eased her hands inside, over a lightly-furred chest. The pecs were rounded with muscle, his six-pack abs evident under her fingers.

"Take it off me." His quiet command sent need rippling all over her. Her pussy was dripping wet.

She removed his shirt but before she could let it drop to the floor, he took it from her. In a blink, he had the cloth twisted into a rope and her wrists bound before her.

She looked up at him in surprise. "Aiden."

"I play dirty and I won't pretend to do otherwise. Tell me if you can't handle it now, Amaryllis."

Her heart fluttered. Played dirty? As in, domination? It seemed that way.

She'd never had anything but vanilla sex, and this side of Aiden definitely hadn't entered her fantasies of the previous night. But now… she couldn't think of anything but letting him take control.

With her breaths rushing out in harsh pants, she felt herself nod. He probably couldn't even see her. "I can handle it," she whispered.

An animalistic noise sounded in his throat. She leaned into him, and he moved her bound arms to circle his neck. As he slammed his mouth over hers, he worked open her jeans. She tensed as his fingertips brushed the top of her mound. She kept her curls trim, but maybe he liked his women bare.

His growl told her otherwise. "Fuck, I wish I could see you. All of you."

"You're wondering if the rug matches the curtains," she said faintly.

His chest rumbled in a laugh. "Crossed my mind. I'll find out later." He pushed her jeans and panties down her hips and cupped her pussy.

In the faint light, his face was carved from granite. She went on tiptoe and pressed light kisses along his chiseled jaw. He moaned and stroked a fingertip over the seam of her pussy, dragging through her juices and spreading them over her swollen bud.

As his mouth enveloped hers in a deep, sucking kiss, he strummed her clit. Over and over, using his whole hand to massage her folds and stimulate absolutely every bit of her sex.

Cream flooded his fingers. "Oh God, Aiden."

"Knew you'd be wet for me."

"Well, I knew you'd be hard for me."

"I'm going to fuck you so hard, you'll be wet thinking about it tomorrow." He doubled the efforts of his fingers.

She bit into his lower lip, and he bit back. She rocked into his hand, and he pinched her nipples with his other. Need spiked. Her core began to pulsate so hard that it rattled her. She forgot where they were and that she shouldn't be letting her colleague touch her this way. Thinking she only needed release.

Now.

From this beautiful, stubborn, straight-laced lawman with the mysterious pain behind his eyes.

"Come for me, doll. Come now." His demand burrowed deep in her psyche. She came.

On demand.

Waves washed over her, shaking her until he supported her fully as he fingered her through her first orgasm in his arms.

Before she'd come down entirely, he pulled out his fingers and trailed the wetness over her lips. She moaned at the newness of the action.

"Taste yourself. Taste how much you want me." He poised his fingertips at her lips, and she parted to let her tongue slide over them.

Sweet juices hit her tongue, and then Aiden's tongue filled her mouth too, swirling over his wet fingers and her tongue simultaneously. She couldn't take it anymore — she needed to touch him.

"Untie me. I need to feel you."

"No. I'm in the driver's seat." He pulled her bound arms over his head and knelt to remove her boots and the rest of her clothes.

* * * * *

With the flavors of Amaryllis's release on his tongue, he had no idea how he was holding it together. The need to claim her roughly, the way he craved, was a hot coal in his groin.

Somehow, he managed not to tear any of her garments while stripping her. He kicked off his own clothes and resisted pulling his belt through the loops of his jeans, but damn, he itched to fold the leather on his palm.

Oh, he'd feel her ass under his belt, all right. But not yet.

She stood before him in full glory, and whoooeee, he didn't know how long he'd last. Just looking at her made him five hip thrusts away from blowing his load.

Her eyes were hazy with passion, her skin blotchy in places where he might have gone too rough with her. She was easily marked. He'd have to remember that.

Letting his gaze dip over her breasts to her belly to the triangle of short curls covering her treasure was all the look-don't-touch he was willing to do.

But she was looking her fill.

"Your tattoos are beautiful."

He flexed his shoulders, feeling his skin was suddenly too tight. Every day of his life he was faced with wearing the images that had made him so proud, but he'd failed the forces and his country. At least that was how they painted the picture after his insubordination.

A chill or maybe emotion made Amaryllis shiver, her dainty toes curled into the tile floor. It wasn't the most romantic place he'd ever taken a woman, but he couldn't wait another moment. He stepped up to her. The warmth of her body combined with his to create an inferno.

He raised her bound wrists and placed them around his neck. Looking down into her eyes, his voice found a brand-new gruffness. "You're fucking beautiful."

Her eyelashes swept over her cheeks as she cast her gaze downward. When she looked up into his eyes again, hers were smoldering with a need so enormous that it was like a fist-punch.

"I want you," she whispered.

He stilled, feeling like someone had just thrown a bucket of ice water over him. "Damn. I don't carry condoms." He had no need for them. It wasn't as if he had heated encounters like this. When he took a woman, it was always planned.

"I'm clean," he said.

At the same time, she said, "I'm on the pill."

The smile they shared ratcheted up his desire for Amaryllis. Her smile, the twinkle in her eyes, her damn beauty stunned him. Stopped his heart.

"Guess there's no reason to hold back, Roshannon."

He leaned close. "Say my name."

"Aiden." The word came out as a breath.

He lifted her, and she wrapped her thighs around him, anchoring her heels above his buttocks. With a growl of hunger, he took her lips.

One smooth shove and he was balls deep. Home.

A gasping cry left her. He swallowed the sound and angled his head to plunge his tongue deeper into her sweet mouth. She was soaking for him, liquid heat engulfing and stealing his goddamned mind.

He rocked his hips back, withdrawing. She shimmied down on his cock again. Holy hell, he'd never had a woman take what she wanted in the first minute they'd been joined. But Amaryllis was strong, independent and still sexy as hell. Even if she was breaking his rules and not giving him all the control, it felt too fucking good to stop her.

He cupped her backside, the cheeks overflowing his hands perfectly, as he ground his hips again. Such a spankable ass.

Her pussy tightened around him, and he hissed with ecstasy on the withdrawal. "You need a good fucking, don't you, baby?" he whispered hotly against her lips.

"No. I need a *great* fucking."

He smiled against her mouth and felt hers twist upward too. "Guess I'd better make it a fucking fantastic fucking."

"Less talk, more action." She jerked her heels, yanking him against her. The head of his cock was burrowed deep inside her warm, slick heat. His balls tightened. He caught her hair in his fist and drew her head back to suck on the spot where her pulse throbbed. Under his tongue, it tripped faster.

He churned his hips and she writhed in his arms. Need claimed his mind, and he stopped thinking. Sensation drove him faster, harder. She cried out and he dipped his head to capture one nipple between his teeth. Biting down as gently as he could when he was this far gone.

She squeezed his length tight with her inner muscles and then she was coming, shaking apart.

One look at the bliss on her face and he was shooting jet after jet deep into her pussy. His roar echoed off the walls, and her sweet rasping cries tore through him.

He wasn't done with her. Not remotely.

Chapter Nine

Amaryllis didn't know if she was on a high or had hit a new low. Contrary to Aiden's beliefs, she *did* have a code of rules. And she'd tossed out every one she'd ever made to protect herself.

No sleeping with people she worked with.

Well, that was blown to hell, wasn't it?

She wiggled in the driver's seat, feeling the aftereffects of him being inside her. Stretching her.

On their way back to Crossroads, he'd asked her to stop at the mini-mart so he could run in and grab something. She had a sneaking suspicion it could be condoms. But why bother now? His release still leaked from her to wet her panties.

Eyes trained on the front of the mini-mart, she started ticking off all the reasons why this affair was a terrible idea. There were plenty, starting with compromising their working relationship and ending with her going home to Texas.

No good could come out of this.

Through the glass doors of the store, she could see Aiden standing at the counter, turned away from her, his hat moving slightly as he nodded at something the clerk said. They stood there for another long minute, and Amaryllis wondered what they could be discussing. Maybe the size of condoms he'd purchased.

A half-snort, half-giggle escaped her, and she shook her head at herself. Aiden Roshannon definitely lived up to the old saying about the bigger the cowboy boots, the bigger the —

He walked out of the store, a white bag in hand and two bottled waters tucked between the fingers of his other. When he jumped into the truck, he eyed her. "Tell me this truck is just a passing fancy of yours to get under my skin."

She put it in reverse and twisted to see while backing up. "Nope. Get used to it."

"Tomorrow I drive."

She straightened out the wheel and drove forward. "We'll take turns. What's in the bag? Is that hot dogs I smell?"

His brows shot upward. "Hot dogs? Woman, that is an insult to this part of the country. These aren't just *hot dogs*. They're triple cheese chili dogs with all the fixin's."

"Sounds like a fantastic meal to eat on the road."

He opened the bag and delved in. Coming out with a foil-wrapped dog cradled in one hand as if it was the Holy Grail. He held it out to her. "Can you drive this monster and still eat?"

"Give me that." She snagged it from his fingers and tore open the foil. The scents of peppers, nacho cheese and chili hit her. "Is this some kind of test? See if Amaryllis's stomach is as cast iron as her personality?"

He chuckled and bit off a chunk of his own. "Sure, if you're up to the challenge."

She eyed him. "Are you serious?"

"Nah, I just wanted a chili dog. And you know my rule of never passing a spot to get food."

She nibbled at the bun, her mind working away from what she and Aiden had done and on to what they'd discovered in the grocery store.

Aiden polished off his first hot dog and crinkled the paper in his fist. He reached into the bag again. "You know I'm not going to let you off the hook for breaking into that building."

She swung her gaze his way, heat creeping into her cheeks, to her horror. "I'm not going to

174

apologize to anybody for anything I do on a case. Everyone knows I have unconventional ways of bagging criminals. Latchaw knew it when he asked me to come to Wyoming."

"Lucky for you that window went right back in. Almost as if you've done that before and you knew it would."

She stared at the road and took a huge mouth full of chili dog to avoid answering.

"Seriously, Amaryllis. I won't stand for that again." He cracked open a bottled water and held it out to her.

She set the hot dog on the console between them and grabbed the water. "Won't stand for it? Am I under your control now?"

His dark stare sent a pulse of need straight between her legs. That look said she was — at least when it came to sex. His shirt was slightly wrinkled from being twisted and knotted around her wrists, which only made the man look more fucking hot and rugged as hell.

"We gotta play by the rules, Amaryllis."

"Is fucking me while on a lead by the rules?" she threw back at him.

He gulped too much water and had to clear his throat hard.

"Did you write that detail in your little notebook, Roshannon?"

"Now that you mention it, I should." He got out his notebook and pen. What he wrote was anybody's guess—she was focusing on her chili dog. Maybe she'd have bad enough breath that he wouldn't want to kiss her again.

After a minute, he slipped the book back into his breast pocket. She held out her hand with the crumpled foil of her hot dog on her palm. He plucked it up and dropped it back into the bag.

"I'll take the other one now."

He laughed. "You sure your stomach's up to it?"

"You don't know a lot about me, Roshannon. But I'll tell you one. My momma always said I could go out and graze with the cows and not have a hint of stomach trouble. Now hand over that dog."

* * * * *

Aiden tossed his notebook down on the coffee table in his living room. The surface was littered with clutter—bills and junk mail as well as receipts for feed he'd purchased and had sent to Eagle Crest to help out with the expenses. Judd was strapped for cash since he'd lost his ass in the divorce, and Aiden could afford to pick up a bit more of the slack for his brother.

Aiden sank to the sagging sofa and stared into space.

After returning to the office to discuss their findings with Latchaw, Aiden had spent some time trying to combine the clues in his head. On the surface, it seemed like two separate crimes, but he and Amaryllis believed the killings and thefts were all connected. If not stemming from one man then by a group of them who all worked together.

Amaryllis had hijacked a computer and spent the entire afternoon doing research. She'd found the cattle brand that had been seared over Owens' wasn't registered anywhere. It was new, fabricated to throw off suspicion.

He stared at his notebook with no new entries to tell him what was going on with the crimes. And it sure didn't tell him what to do about this ache inside—the one he had for a feisty little strawberry blonde with the constitution of a US Marine.

Hell, if she'd been given the order to fire upon that bunker, she probably could have done it. Far as he could tell, she didn't hesitate on anything ever. Eat one of Crossroads' mini-mart death dogs? Hand it over. Remove a windowpane and climb through the window without knowing the danger on the other side? Hell yeah.

Buck against his cock to find her release? Oh fuck yes.

He sat back on the couch and threaded his fingers through his hair, but all he felt was Amaryllis's silky strands. The bright locks that intrigued the hell out of him. He wanted to see it twisted in his fist as he marked her ass with his palm prints.

He threw a glance at the clock on the wall. It was well past eleven. Would she be sleeping?

Did he care? She wasn't the only person who could run with her urges.

He stood and jammed his hat back on his head. He cast a look around his lonely living room. The sagging furniture and clutter didn't require attention. All he had to do was walk out and lock the door behind him.

Five minutes later, he stood at Amaryllis's door. The B&B owner had let him in with a wink that was probably relief that Aiden wasn't here for her daughter.

He rapped lightly on the wooden door. Inside, he heard a rustling sound. Was she throwing on clothes? *No need.*

When she opened the door, she was fully dressed, sans boots and hat. Her hair floating loose and her eyes bright. "Aiden." His name came out as a breath. "What are you doing here?"

"Can I come in?" He met her gaze.

Her lips parted. "Is that a good idea?"

"Depends on how quiet you can be while I rock your world, Amaryllis. Now make your choice."

She threw a look past him and then stepped back to let him pass into her room. She hurried to close the door and lock it. Then she leaned against it as if in need of the support. His own body felt mighty jelly-like, so he understood.

They stared at each other for a long heartbeat. Suddenly, she lunged into his arms at the same moment he scooped her up. Their mouths collided with a primal need. His cock stiffened in a blink and she practically shimmied up him like a pole.

He lifted her under her ass and broke from the kiss long enough to say, "I'm takin' you in a bed this time."

"And after that?" She worked at his buttons while pressing nipping bites to his throat.

"After that, we have some options." The bed was piled with pillows and quilts, and a silky robe lay across the foot. He threw her down and crawled atop her.

She stared up at him, chest heaving. "What options?"

"Well," he drawled, leaning back enough to peel the top over her head. Her breasts rose up, cradled in black silk bra cups. His mouth dried out, and somehow he managed to get out the rest of his sentence. "There's the shower."

"Mmm." She arched enough to let him slide his hands underneath her and unclasp her bra.

"The sofa."

"How boring." She bit his lower lip hard enough to sting.

Growling, he saw spots for a moment before throttling back the powerful lust inside him again. He had to take this slow.

"It won't be boring when you're bound hand and foot, on your knees, taking the leather of my belt across your round ass."

Her eyes widened and she sucked in a sharp breath. He studied her eyes. Was she aroused or frightened to death?

He waited for some sign that he should go on, that she accepted this dirty side of him and wanted to continue.

She slid her hands inside his shirt, skimming warm fingers over his skin. She found his nipples and tweaked them hard.

A harsh groan issued from him. "Amaryllis, say the word now if you want to stop. Because once I start, I'm not sure I can."

She leaned upward, her lips brushing his. "I want you," she whispered.

With need raging through his system, he tore off her clothes. She unbuckled his belt and jeans and got as far as easing her hand inside his boxers. He gripped her wrist, stopping her.

"I'll tell you when you can touch me."

Her eyelids fluttered. "I want to taste you."

Gulping back a growl, he counted to ten. Backward. Once he had some semblance of control, he said, "I'll feed you my cock as soon as I've had my fill of you." Then ducked his head and sucked her nipple into his mouth.

She bowed off the bed, crying out, her fingers tangled in his hair as he tormented her with hot passes of his tongue. The scent of her arousal flooded him with need, and he didn't know how much longer he could hold back.

He moved to the other nipple, giving it the same bathing with his tongue. "So fucking beautiful even if you're a pain in the ass."

She giggled, and it cut off on a gasp as he ran his tongue down the flat of her stomach toward her pussy. "Such a charmer. I don't know why I'm letting you touch me this way."

He lifted his head and pierced her in his gaze. "Because we're like a cat and dog going at each other. Then at the end of the day, we curl up as friends."

"Is that what you call… this?" She sucked in sharply when his tongue struck wet honeyed gold. He lapped over her clit and down the seam of her pussy to her opening. Juices soaked his tongue, and he swirled it, lapping them up. Tasting her essence, his cock rock hard, barely harnessed by his underwear. Good thing his fly was open—he would have busted the zipper otherwise.

He burrowed his tongue into her folds, dipping into her pussy. Her inner muscles clenched on him, but he withdrew, teasing her. She yanked his hair, and he rumbled his amusement against her sensitive tissues.

One small heel beat the mattress in frustration. "Roshannon!"

"Aiden to you when I'm between your thighs, Amaryllis. Say it."

Her eyes shot dark brown sparks. Whether lust or annoyance, he had no idea. With her, it could swing either way. He ran his tongue to her clit again, circling slowly while she moaned, "Aidennnnn."

* * * * *

182

She'd lost her damn mind, and she'd never get it back at this rate. He was doing things to her clit with his tongue that no man should ever know how to do. Did men even understand a woman's body this way? Aiden seemed to.

He licked in small circles and then spread them wider, like rings rippling on a pond. Her pussy squeezed hard, juices sliding down her body. When he sucked her clit into his mouth using strong pulls, she threw her head back and let her first orgasm sweep over her.

Shaking, her belly muscles jumping. Need lashing her like the spanking he promised to give her with his belt. The thought only shot her higher, wringing more contractions out of her.

When he raised his head, she met his stare. His eyes were hazy with passion, and damn if she didn't want to see him in the same throes of ecstasy she'd just been in.

She grabbed his shoulders and guided him back up. His kiss was wet with her release and he shared her flavors for long seconds. "My turn," she whispered.

He clutched her wrist and moved her hand over his cock. "Can you take that in your mouth all the way?"

He was big. Maybe not. "I want to."

"Get on your hands and knees."

She rolled slowly over, trying to find equilibrium after that mind-shattering orgasm. Wetness leaked down her inner thighs as she assumed the position he'd commanded her to get into.

He moved to his feet at the side of the bed, and never shifting his eyes off her, stripped his clothes off. She watched the way his hands moved, veins snaking down his forearms. His eyes smoldered, and her breath was coming too fast. Dizziness hit her, and she had to slow her breaths to keep from hyperventilating.

He didn't move toward her, even when she wet her lips invitingly.

He seemed content to stand there looking at her.

"Arch your back for me, doll."

Dear God, was she seriously taking commands from a man this way? She was a strong woman, and she was letting him treat her like a plaything.

Yet she fucking loved every minute of it.

She arched her back, breasts thrusting up, ass in the air.

"More."

A shiver ran through her. "Like… this?"

"Good." That single word wove through her psyche. The praise something she hadn't known she craved until right this minute. On the surface, Aiden Roshannon was a man who liked to be in control, but she'd never guessed he was like this in the bedroom.

"Now wet your lips. Run your tongue over them." His gaze locked to her mouth.

Feeling strangely confident under his stare, she did his bidding, teasing him with her movement.

He grunted, and she felt a heady wave of power at how she was affecting him. Her nipples felt so heavy, aching for his touch and the bite of his teeth.

He cupped his balls in one hand and fisted the base of his impressive length with the other. As he stepped up to the bed, knees digging into the mattress, he ran his cock head over her lips. Back and forth, smearing his pre-cum over them.

She stuck out her tongue and lapped at the juices, pulling another rough moan from him. When he eased the tip of his cock into her mouth, she closed her eyes to savor the warm velvety steel on her tongue. He pushed deeper.

"Look at me. I want to see your eyes as I work into your throat."

Jesus, this was really happening. His dirty talk meshed with her submission sent her whirling with bone-melting desire.

He pushed deeper, gliding on her tongue all the way to the back of her throat. "Angle your head, doll. That's it." He edged farther in.

She swallowed on reflex, and he snapped his hands into fists. Was he battling for control? She swore she felt his shaft pulsating, ready to explode. But a man like Aiden wouldn't let that happen. He'd get everything he wanted from her and then some.

"Now suck."

She squeezed her thighs together as he fucked in and out of her mouth. She hollowed her cheeks. He closed his eyes and bucked into her for several more strokes before yanking free.

"You're fucking good at that. Great. Too fucking great." He clamped the head of his cock in one fist as he placed a knee on the bed. "Keep your ass in the air. Like that, yes. Fuck."

He was speaking in short, jerky bursts, testimony that he was close to losing it. She reached back and caught his hip, pulling him to her. He moaned as his cock slipped easily into her soaking pussy.

"Fucking hell, you're so hot and wet." He sank balls deep.

* * * * *

186

Sweat dripped down Aiden's temple as he battled for self-control. He wanted to take it slow, but Amaryllis wasn't having any of it. She pushed him to the brink. He swore if she tightened around him one more time, he'd —

He clenched his jaw and breathed through his nose. In for five, out for five. Her long hair trailed down her spine, caressing her pale skin. At her throat, her pulse flickered. He ducked his head and placed his mouth over that spot, tasting sweet woman and the tang of her own perspiration dewed on her skin.

"Take me, Aiden. Don't hold back."

He swallowed. "You don't want me to let go, doll."

She squeezed his fingers digging into her hip. "I know what I'm asking for."

Ffffuck. Did she?

He gave an answering rock of his hips, burrowing his cock against the entrance of her womb. She cried out. He withdrew slowly, lapping circles around her rapidly-beating pulse point with his tongue. Anything to distract himself.

But she felt so fucking amazing, clenching around him so perfectly, like she'd been made for this.

For him.

Hell, he was thinking of having her as a permanent fixture in his bed. It happened that way for some. He had a buddy in the military who'd come home on leave, met a girl and married her the same week. They were still happily married, last he'd heard.

But then there was Judd. His twin had been head over boots for Cassie, and in the end, she'd left him broken. He refused to speak of it, so Aiden knew it pained him.

Was he on the same slippery path, falling in lust with the first woman who'd stimulated his brain *and* his libido? He wasn't lookin' for more than a taste of the stunning woman. And maybe to shut her up for a bit.

He grinned at that and slid deep into her pussy again. She hung forward in his arms, rasping her pleasure as he fucked her with slow, measured movements. As he bottomed out, she'd push back and grind. The sweetest torture in the universe.

He lashed an arm around her middle and held her fast to his body. "You think you want my belt on your backside."

"I do." She whimpered as he pulled out almost to the tip.

"What about my palm? My paddle? Can you stand it if I tie you up and blindfold you and make you take me into your throat?"

She breathed out in a rush. Then nodded. "Yes."

"Fuck, Amaryllis." He knew her well enough to realize she wasn't easily frightened. Maybe—just maybe—she *could* handle him. So far, she hadn't backed down from anything he'd thrown at her, even the commands.

He stroked her breasts with one hand while inching the other down her body. He cupped her pussy hard, applying pressure to her clit. She was swollen, and he knew if he had that little bundle of nerves beneath his tongue, he'd feel it pulse as if with its own heartbeat.

"Oh God, Aiden. Yesss."

He massaged her pussy as he fucked her faster. She was climbing, juices slicking his cock and creating a soft sucking noise.

"You can't come until I say you can."

"I can't hold back."

He deliberately slowed, edging her away from the cliff of pleasure. In her ear, he rumbled, "You only come when I say so."

"Please. Aiden!"

He stroked her clit, trapping it between his fingers and rubbing up and down. He pushed into her body again and felt her contract. So close.

"Focus on my voice, doll. Only on me, not what your body's telling you to do."

"I don't know if I can." Her voice trembled.

"If you pass this test, I'll reward you. Generously. Now listen to me. Do not come."

She seemed to still in his arms and he continued to torment her with his cock and fingers. Drawing deep moans from her that grew more guttural with every caress. Her body shook.

How far could he push? He couldn't have her losing faith in him, but he had to know her limits and take her half a step beyond.

She clamped down on his cock, and need flooded his body, pressure on his lower spine increasing. His balls aching to blow.

"Easy, doll. That's it. Listen to me now. You want to come."

"Yes!"

"You're so close."

"Oh my God. Fuck."

He grinned. Dirty mouth and all, she was a gem.

"Feel my cock glide into your pussy. Tighten your muscles around it."

She obeyed, limp, breathing hard.

"Now feel your clit under my finger. So swollen."

She cried out. She couldn't go on much longer.

He lifted his fingers from her body one by one until he was no longer touching her. She trembled against him.

"Think of my fingers there." He pushed in hard.

"Yes!"

"Now come, Amaryllis. Come on my cock."

She did with a scream of pleasure that probably rattled the windows of the rest of the B&B. He fucked her fast as she clenched and released around him. He issued a growl, cum rushed up his shaft. The first splash on her inner walls made her tighten around him again.

He pounded into her, stars bursting in his vision. But all he could think was that he'd fucking achieved more with her in one short session than any of his lovers had with him after months.

Not many could be his lover, as submissive as he needed.

But Amaryllis was.

Chapter Ten

"They just finished questioning Fitz. He wasn't anywhere near Brown's place last night," Amaryllis said as she stuffed her phone in her pocket.

Aiden threw her a look. "How do they know?"

"Because he spent the night in jail in the next county for drunk driving."

So he couldn't be responsible for the crime they were about to investigate. Ed Brown's place was on the county border and during the entire drive here—in Aiden's truck—he'd wanted to reach over and feel up Amaryllis's leg. She was doing her best to keep their relationship all business, though.

Her sweet ass swayed with every step she took across Brown's ranch.

"Holy fuck," Aiden said as they walked a bit farther and he spotted the entrails of a cow, a bloody, gruesome streak that led to the carcass.

Amaryllis sped ahead of him and bent to stare at the ground. She was most likely checking for tracks. The ground was muddy and bloody. There had to be some evidence left behind. Trouble was, in these parts, everybody wore boots that were purchased at the same store in Crossroads. They all left behind the same tracks.

The rancher's face was grim as he stared at the loss of his cattle. At least thirteen-hundred dollars butchered right here in his field. A big loss.

Aiden asked him some questions to nail down the timeline while Amaryllis circled the bloody scene, sometimes peering close at something. Once she used a forefinger to probe a bit on the carcass.

Aiden watched her closely while trying to keep his mind on his conversation. He could see the woman's brain working, and damn if he didn't want to hear what was going on inside it.

"We'll take some pictures and then help you clear this mess," Aiden said to the rancher.

He rubbed his craggy jaw and nodded. Loss was always hard, even to seasoned ranchers like Brown. "Appreciate it."

Moving to Amaryllis's side, Aiden felt her start as if she hadn't realized he was even there. When she looked up at him, her eyes were far away.

"What are your thoughts?" he asked, low.

"Whoever did this has a taste for more than beef or selling beef. He took the heart."

He straightened. "You sure?" He went to the carcass and stared down at the place the heart would be.

Sure enough, the big arteries were severed.

"This is fucking sick," he said before he could stop herself.

"Really fucking sick. It's almost like a ritual, isn't it?" Her voice was thoughtful.

Aiden's skin prickled, but no way was he going to admit that to anyone, least of all Amaryllis, who seemed completely unfazed by the gruesome detail. "Or it could just be a man who's got a taste for heart. Some do." Hell, his pa did. He liked it cooked nice and slow so it was tender.

Amaryllis chewed her lower lip, white teeth moving over the plump tissue. His cock stirred.

The rancher walked over to pull a shovel out of the back of his pickup.

"Take the photos, Roshannon. I'm going to check the woods."

He threw her a look. "Alone? Like hell."

Her brow crinkled. "Why the hell not? You think the guy who butchered this cow is lurking in the woods waiting to leap out and attack me?"

He flexed his shoulders. Put that way, it sounded unlikely, silly even. But he didn't like the thought of her going off on her own.

"You're not going alone."

Her eyes narrowed. "What is this? Some odd show of protection toward me? Just because your dick was inside me doesn't mean you need to protect me."

Glaring, he stepped up to her, so close that her body heat washed over him. Her beautiful face was twisted in annoyance, and damn if he didn't want to kiss her pretty mouth.

"I'll go with you. End of story."

"Good Lord, Roshannon."

He shot her a deadly look at the use of his last name. "What happened to Aiden? Last night you were panting my name, begging my name, screaming my name."

She set her hands on her hips, eyes shooting bullets. "I knew I should never had let you touch me. Damn fool doesn't know when to separate work from pleasure," she muttered.

He reached out and slid a tendril of her hair behind her ear. "What I do know is you aren't going to those woods alone. I know you want to look for ATV tracks."

"Of course I do." She batted his hand away from her face.

"We are a team. We stick together."

"Meaning you think I'm incapable of going alone because you filled me with your cum." Her voice was pitched low, furious.

He grabbed her waist, anchoring her in front of him in case she wanted to move away. "You're more than capable, Amaryllis. But maybe I want to go with you because you're starting to mean something to me."

She went dead still, all but her jaw, which dropped. She stared up at him. A heartbeat passed in silence.

He released her waist. "We'll go in a minute. Let me take some photos."

To his surprise, she waited for him. He wasn't one to dominate outside the bedroom, but when it came to her safety, he would damn well take the upper hand. At this point, the crimes were getting closer together and the rustler obviously bold and uncaring of his moves.

After taking the photos, the rancher began to dig the hole to bury the remains. Amaryllis took off for the woods. Aiden kept stride with her.

"I can't lie. I want to throw you against one of these trees and have my way with you."

She shook her head. "We're on the job."

"Didn't say I was going to. Not yet, anyway. I have a little self-control."

"You have a lot." She checked herself as if she hadn't meant to say that at all. "Stop grinning, Roshannon." She emphasized his last name, separating business from pleasure.

"Just remember—we have an hour in the truck together to get to that slaughterhouse. We'll be all alone."

"Shut up."

The path the ATV had taken was evident, the underbrush compressed under tires. Well, now they knew how the rustler had made away with the beef.

"Latchaw's got patrol on that grocery store. They didn't see anything last night or this morning?" he asked Amaryllis.

She'd been on the phone with the sheriff for half an hour during the drive. All her knowledge of the topic of the law had been like foreplay, had driven him crazy. He wanted her then—and now more than ever.

She shook her head. "Not a thing. They didn't butcher it there. Has to be another place. I wonder…"

"What are you thinkin'?" he asked.

"Owens' neighbor. Jack Mitchell."

He studied her eyes. "We've agreed we believe there's two crimes taking place here—

those stealing and selling the live cattle. And those selling the meat they steal."

She nodded.

"We need to visit the local slaughterhouse, see if anybody's brought in meat in the last six hours." They'd been checking daily.

"Right. Then it's easy enough to get a search warrant for Mitchell's place."

"Guess your plans to ravish me in the truck on the way to the slaughterhouse are on hold, Roshannon. We're making a trip over to Mitchell's first."

"Plenty of places to pull off." His voice came out gritty.

She cocked a brow at him. "Keep it in your pants for now, lawman. We've got work to do."

* * * * *

After Aiden's comment about her starting to mean something to him, Amaryllis had hardly listened to the rest of the conversation. Other than he wanted to fuck her. *That* was one thing her body had heard loud and clear.

She felt off-balance. And she was never off-balance.

He didn't know nearly enough about her to feel something besides lust and, she knew, disapproval at her tactics when it came to

198

getting her rustler. Hell, they were practically strangers.

Strangers who know how to make each other feel amazing.

Spending long days with the man made her feel they'd worked together much longer. She had to admit, he was growing on her. Even the sight of his stupid little book made her feel a warm wave of affection. Though she didn't know nearly enough about Aiden Roshannon, she knew he was a good man and was driven by his work ethic, same as her.

She'd had partners in the past, but none of them lasted long. Technically, he wouldn't either. As soon as they solved the case, she'd return to Texas.

The whole way to Mitchell's, her thoughts ran between Aiden and the case. There were a lot more missing pieces than she wanted. They needed to work harder, longer hours. Forego sleep and... other things... if they had to. Getting the criminals was most important.

She dragged in a deep breath. Aiden's fresh piney scent filled the truck cab and even clung to her.

He switched on the radio. "Do you mind?"

She shook her head.

"Helps me think. Takes my mind off the obvious parts of the case and sometimes things come to me."

She nodded. "We need to get one of these guys to talk. Give us names."

"Sheriff Mead's good at putting the pressure on a man. He'll have Fitz singing in no time."

The dulcet tones of a country music singer projected through the speakers, and Aiden sang along. She stared at him, unable to stop the chills that ran up and down her body at the beauty of his deep voice.

She couldn't stop hearing his commands either. *Take off your clothes. Open your mouth. Arch your back. Don't come until I say so.*

Giving him control in the bedroom was something she'd never expected could be such a turn-on. She wanted more of it. All those promised spankings. And the rope. She *was* a cowgirl at heart, after all.

He stopped singing, staring out the windshield, deep in thought. She didn't interrupt the silence in case he was working over some good tidbit of the crime, though how he was doing it without scribbling in his book was anybody's guess.

After a spell, he shot her a smile. "Hope my singin' wasn't too terrible."

"The opposite. You're very good. I didn't know you can sing."

The corner of his lips tipped up. "Doesn't say that in my file? I know you went through it."

"Williams told you."

"That deputy only keeps quiet about cases. But when it comes to office gossip, he sings like a canary."

She laughed. "So while we're on the subject of what your file didn't reveal, can I ask you a few questions?"

His eyes were the darkest gray. "Guess it's only fair that you get to know me, since we work so closely."

She tried to form her words in a way that wouldn't put him on instant defensive. But she knew what she wanted to ask would do that anyway.

"Out with it, Amaryllis. You're not one to hold your tongue."

"Thanks."

"You don't need to sound so cheerful about that. It wasn't exactly a compliment."

"Is to me. I pride myself in saying what I mean."

He chuckled. "Lay it on me, then." His low tone suggested he meant something besides her questions.

"I wondered about your time in the military."

He sobered, and she noted the change in his posture, shoulders tense as if someone had tightened the muscle stretching between them. "What about it?" His tone wasn't angry, but it was guarded.

"I read something that pointed to the fact that you *didn't* follow a command. That surprises me."

"Yeah, well, I'm by the book now."

"Is that why?"

He swung his stare to her. Warmth bloomed in her stomach, and it had nothing to do with sex. It had to do with affection for this man.

"There's times to follow the rules and times to break 'em."

"They gave you a command you couldn't execute, didn't they?"

"It's all classified information, so I can't tell you any specifics. But let's say their command went against the grain. For that, I was shipped back to the States and spent several days being questioned. Almost court marshalled. Didn't think I'd get a place in the law like I did, but people around here know me and they gave me a chance."

"I can tell you're an important part of the sheriff's department. And all these ranchers rely on you."

"On you too." He met her stare.

"Glad to do my part," she said. "Although, I must admit, this case is taking a bit longer than usual. It's pretty involved."

"Lots of people we need to speak to. I've been thinking we should haul in all of Mitchell's and Fitz's friends and family members. Interrogate them in one spot."

"That could work, but your office's mighty small for that."

He chuckled. "That it is. I was thinking we need to hook up with Judd. Find out what he's heard. Rumors have a way of spreading across counties."

"Would we go to him?"

"I was thinkin' halfway. Eagle Crest."

He'd take her to his family home—to meet his twin, his parents? Amaryllis gripped the seat. What did that mean? Somehow, Aiden's tone didn't make her think it was only business on his mind.

"What do you say?" he asked.

"Anything for the case."

He nodded thoughtfully and turned back to the windshield.

In minutes, they reached Mitchell's place. A truck was parked in the driveway and the dogs were milling around. When the animals saw them pull in, they rushed the truck.

"Let me handle this." Aiden gave her a steely look.

"I'll take care of the dogs. You talk to Nicky. And Mitchell if he's here."

"Here's here, all right. It's just a matter of finding the man." He got out of the truck.

Amaryllis soothed the dogs, who seemed to remember her. They let her scratch their ears and pet their heads as they circled both her and Aiden all the way to the front door, their barks deafening.

This time Aiden opened the door.

She stared at him. "Are you serious? You can't just open the door," she mocked.

He arched a brow at her and called into the house, "Hello!"

Nicky rushed into the front room, hands wet as if she'd been washing dishes or scrubbing something.

Amaryllis stared at her hands. At a bloody little finger.

"How dare you walk into my home again?" Nicky shot out.

"The deputy will be arriving any second with the search warrant." He cocked his head at the crunch of gravel outside. "There he is now. We'd like to have a look around. If you fight us, you'll be taken into custody."

Nicky paled. Amaryllis kept her gaze trained on that pinky finger. It *was* blood, but it wasn't *bleeding*. Not a cut.

She took a step toward the woman. Aiden made a noise in his chest, and she knew his protective instincts were rising up again, but he'd have to choke on them for the time being. She had a job to do.

"You've got some blood," she said to the woman.

She looked down at her hands as if wondering how they were even attached to her arms. "I... cut myself. I was chopping vegetables for soup."

Amaryllis made a sympathetic sound in her throat. "Let's see if we can find you a Band-Aid." She took Nicky by the arm and led her into the kitchen while the deputy entered with the warrant and he and Aiden started sweeping the house.

When Amaryllis got Nicky into the kitchen, there wasn't a vegetable in sight. Not surprising. There was, however, a nice-sized cut of beef on the counter.

She turned to Nicky. "Don't lie to me and things'll go easier for you. We know your man's involved in some illegal activity, and if you tell us all about it, the charges against you will be lighter or even dropped altogether. Especially if he's forcing you to help him. By hurting you?"

She looked into Nicky's eyes.

The woman shifted her gaze away.

"You realize Special Investigator Roshannon and I are looking into some cattle slaughters in this area. Some of your neighbor's beef's gone missing too."

"Heard he got those back."

"Not all of them. And just this morning we were down at the bottom of the county looking at a cow that was killed, butchered where it lay. Even the heart was taken. You know anything about that?" Amaryllis leaned against the counter. The slab of beef lay there inches away.

"Interesting, this cut. Doesn't look as if it was cut with a meat saw. Looks more ragged, like someone used a big knife. Don't you think?"

Nicky went to the kitchen sink and washed her hands quickly and then dried them on a dishtowel. "I wouldn't know about that."

"Did you purchase this beef? Maybe at Willy's?"

She knew damn well Willy's was the grocery that was out of business, where she and Aiden had made a discovery… and more.

"Willy's ain't been open for a while now."

"Then where'd you get it?"

"The only other place to get a good cut of beef is up at Siverly's."

"Oh, they deal in cuts of beef like this?" Amaryllis's tone had Nicky hesitating. As if the woman knew what she asked, or at least the implication of it.

"It's a simple question, Nicky."

She nodded.

"I'll let you get back to cutting so you can get this beef in the freezer. Can't let it spoil." She pulled away from the counter and walked into the other room. Deputy Williams stood at the door, watching something that was taking place on the porch. A dog snarled.

Amaryllis stepped up next to Williams, and the deputy looked down at her with a slow, crooked smile. "Looks as if Mitchell finally showed his face."

"Yeah, to the wrong man."

Mitchell was in cuffs, clothes stained in blood as if something big, maybe a cow, had bled all over him, while Aiden read him his Miranda rights.

Chapter Eleven

By the time Aiden and Amaryllis finished questioning Mitchell, they had the law from several counties involved in the case. Amaryllis had spent an hour on the phone with a constable near Laramie who'd heard of some tainted beef coming into a local grocery and a case had been opened because so many people were getting sick.

In trying to slide the attention from himself and his involvement in the butchering, Mitchell had told them something about a guy with a suspicious cattle brand that had Amaryllis on the phone again, this time with a brand investigator in Cheyenne.

She appeared in the door of the interrogation room again, eyes bright. "False brand not affiliated with any ranch in Wyoming or the neighboring states. Several cows sold off last week, calves too. We found out who bought the cows and the Cheyenne sheriff's office is sending someone down there now to investigate."

Mitchell looked up with hope on his face. "I can tell you more."

"You *will* tell us more—everything you know," Aiden said slowly, with deadly calm in his voice. "Starting with how you got involved in this. A family man like you, working hard to support his family as a mechanic."

He was playing to the man's morals to get him to discuss the crimes.

Mitchell nodded. Amaryllis came to sit next to Aiden, her thigh so close he could feel the warmth off it. The urge to let his knee fall to the side and brush his leg against hers was strong, but he resisted.

As soon as he got her alone, though, he wasn't playing around. No holding back. He had a length of rope in his truck that would serve well.

They wrung a bit more from Mitchel, but half an hour later, the man had clammed up.

Aiden stood and motioned to Williams to come into the room. "Show him to his new home."

Williams nodded and went to hook a hand around Mitchell's biceps. "Come with me. I'll show you what a cell looks like."

As soon as the man was out of the room, Aiden looked into Amaryllis's eyes. She shook her head. "He didn't tell us much. Protecting someone. Or he's scared."

"I'd say scared. Did you see how sweat broke out on his forehead when we started really asking questions?"

She nodded.

"What's on your mind? I see you're thinkin' on somethin'."

"I was thinking we need to start asking the local businesses who's coming in and making unusual purchases. Electronics store. Off-roading vehicles."

Damn, she was one smart little cookie. "You're right. If someone's suddenly got money, he's going to spend it. C'mon. Let's grab a little lunch and talk to some people."

"A bit late for lunch, isn't it?"

"Too early for supper. Besides, I plan on having more than one meal today." He gave her a long look that had pink blooming in her cheeks. He ducked his head to cover his smile.

Fifteen minutes later, with a pot of steaming coffee between them and two big meals on order, he and Amaryllis had a brainstorming session about the case. Mitchell had given them a few leads, but now they knew the rustling ring was bigger than they'd believed. It involved several counties and the thieves would be serving real jail time.

Aiden wrote more details in his book but put it away when their food arrived. Amaryllis lifted her fork and tucked into her home fries with onions and green peppers as if she'd been on the trail for days without a hot meal. When she glanced up to find him staring, that pink blush rose to her cheeks once more.

"You're mighty pretty when you blush."

"Shut up, Roshannon."

"I'd like to make you blush all over." He pitched his voice low.

She darted her tongue out and wet her lower lip. "Not here."

"Back at my place then. I think we horrified the owners of the B&B where you're staying enough for one week."

She gulped down her bite in her mouth, looking nervous. Aiden sat back in his seat and studied her. He'd never seen her anything less than perfectly in control of her emotions. But right now, she didn't seem to be able to keep the blush from her face or the excitement from her glances.

He ate his meal with a tight chest and a tighter pair of Wranglers. He wanted her so bad that he couldn't guarantee he'd get her home. The rope *was* in his truck, after all.

After she'd polished off her home fries and a country fried steak, the waitress asked if she could get them slices of fresh banana cream pie. Amaryllis shook her head and Aiden asked for the check. He'd have his pie, all right, but they needed to be alone.

With a hand on her lower back, he guided her out of the restaurant and to the truck. He made a move to reach for her door, but she grabbed the handle first. Throwing a look over her shoulder, she said, "I got this."

He inched closer, trapping her against the steel and his body. Looking down into her eyes, he said, "I love how independent you are, doll. But remember that when I take control, you're going to be begging for more."

Her eyes grew hazy and she opened her mouth to say something. He brushed his lips across hers in a brief kiss and then pushed away from the truck. He got in before she did, and he figured she must be standing there dazed.

Smiling to himself, he headed out on the road, back to the job. They needed to hit the slaughterhouse before the second shift came on and cattle were loaded into the building.

"Aiden." Her voice came hesitantly.

He fixed her in his gaze. "Yeah, doll."

She locked her fingers together and a flush crept over her throat. "I think we should talk about what we're going to do. Later, I mean. With you dominating me."

His cock stretched to full hardness in one word — dominating.

He slowed the truck to a speed he felt more comfortable keeping while talking about how he was going to pleasure her and with a raging hard-on. "What do you know about domination?"

A shiver ran through her. "Not much. Just things you hear."

"Like what?" He already knew. The misconceptions around BDSM were widespread and rampant. People believed it was about pain when really it was about trust.

She lifted a shoulder in an adorable shrug. "Just that the... spankings... are sometimes painful."

"Depends on who's doing it. If done right, you'll feel the sting but be so consumed by the passion and need that you won't give it a thought."

"And you're... good at it?"

"Been told I am. Amaryllis, there's something we both get in the deal, and that's pleasure. If you're not feeling that, then we stop. Period." She wouldn't want that, though. By asking questions, she was already receptive, and he'd seen the rapture on her face while obeying his commands.

"I've heard there's a safe word." She threw him a look, eyes feverish, cheeks pink.

God, he wanted to strip her clothes off here and now and find that rope.

He managed to grip the wheel and nod. "Yes, you choose the word. One that means something to you but that you wouldn't just use in a conversation."

"I-I read that a lot of people use the word Oklahoma."

He blinked. "Oklahoma?"

"Yeah, it's on the top fifteen list of safe words in the US."

"You researched this?"

"Yes."

"When?" He was amused, aroused and ready to rumble.

"I looked it up on my phone while I was waiting for information from those constables in Laramie."

He hit the brakes and stopped in the middle of the road. Not much traffic out this way, and they weren't causing a hazard. But Amaryllis's admission was sure wreaking havoc with his libido.

"Let me get this straight. While you were working a case, you were thinking of me?" He pitched his voice low, holding her gaze. "Thinking of me taking you into my bedroom and knotting my rope around you and spanking your ass?"

Another shiver ripped through her. "Yes."

Damn, he loved how she didn't look away when she answered him. How she was bold in the face of something new. He didn't think there was a single thing on earth she'd back down from.

He reached across the console and wrapped his fingers lightly around her wrist. Her eyelids fluttered as she realized he was simulating a restraint. Her breasts heaved as her breathing came faster.

"And you've decided Oklahoma's your safe word?"

She nodded. "Seems better than some of the other suggestions. Not so basic."

His cock head felt so engorged it would burst. "And what were some of those?"

"Red, stop, banana, pineapple."

He chuckled. "Oklahoma definitely suits you better, doll." He unbuckled his seat belt. Then he leaned across the console, tightening his hold on her wrist as he cupped her jaw and kissed her.

The soft melding of mouths quickly turned into a heated, tongue-questing kiss. Long passes of his tongue through her mouth raised groans from each of them. When he ran his hand over her breast, finding the center as hard as a gumdrop, he bit back a roar.

Hell yeah, this woman wanted him, all of him. The dirty kinky side of him. She hadn't even run when he'd told her about his mess with the military.

He drew back enough to look into her eyes. Her long lashes dipped over her smoldering gaze.

"I want you so fucking bad, Amaryllis." His voice sounded raw, roughened by blazing need.

"I want you too. Is it terrible I want to skip the slaughterhouse and go straight to your place?"

He dropped his forehead to hers with a grunt. Breathing hard, he said, "Let's get this over with so we can play."

She pressed a kiss to the corner of his mouth, a tender caress that did things to his heart as well as his body. When he didn't move, she whispered, "Aiden."

He needed to stop touching her, get back to driving. They'd been sitting in the middle of the road for long minutes. Luckily, the few cars that traveled this way on a regular basis wouldn't be by until evening.

"Aiden, let's get on the road, get it over with like you said."

Unable to move for the ache in his groin and the bigger one swelling around his heart, he continued to cup her face.

Suddenly, she started to belt out, "Oooooooklahoma! Where the wind comes—"

He stamped her mouth hard with his kiss, silencing her. They laughed through the moment and he faced forward and gripped the wheel again.

"At least we know my safe word works." She sounded smug and excited at the same time.

He adjusted his swollen cock but no amount of nudging would ease the throb there. He sent her a look. "That'll be the first and last time you use that word, doll. Because I have no intention of giving you anything but the pleasure you need and deserve. You won't want me to stop."

She bit down on her lower lip and nodded to the window. "Drive, Roshannon."

A grin stretched over his face so wide it made his cheeks hurt. At first, he'd believed himself saddled with a pain in the ass for a partner. Now he couldn't imagine working a case without her.

* * * * *

Aiden's home was set back from the road, a small cabin-like structure with absolutely no cheer or hominess. Amaryllis hadn't been expecting something off the pages of a décor magazine, but the man was so full of life that she couldn't connect him with this space. His cubicle back in the sheriff's office seemed to reflect him more, and it was bleak to say the least.

She couldn't lie to herself and say she wasn't nervous. The prospect of giving up her control completely to Aiden was nerve-wracking. And hot as hell. All day long she'd been thinking of what was to come, and she was in a constant state of arousal, her panties damp.

"Do you have a dog?" she asked.

"With all the long hours I keep, how would I have time for one?"

"I guess I wasn't thinking about that. You seem like a guy who'd like a companion."

"Maybe someday," he said noncommittally.

"I don't have any pets either. I had a fish a few years back, but I went off on a case and forgot to get someone in to feed it or leave one of those vacation feeders. When I came back, it was belly up."

Across the cab, he sent her a long look, the corner of his lips tipped up. "You still beat yourself up over that, don't you, Amaryllis?"

Being thrown together like they were gave them a crash-course in getting to know each other. He seemed to understand things about her that most people didn't. Only her brother, JD knew how bad she'd felt about that fish.

Poor Mr. Guppy.

Aiden stopped the truck in front of the house and cut the engine. A monumental silence took hold of them. He dipped his head, hat concealing his eyes. "If you want to back out, say the word and I'll take you home."

"I don't," she said at once. Her words raspy.

He shot her a smoldering look and then got out of the truck. She sat there a moment, taking in what she was about to do. Putting herself in his hands was a huge deal to her — she was always in control.

We've had hot, kinky sex before.

Not like this will be.

He opened her door. She turned to him and slid out into his waiting arms.

He scooped her against his chest with a growl of need. The fireworks shooting off before they'd taken a single step toward the front door. He swayed her to his body, molding her to fit him. And her body answered with a resounding *hell yeah.*

She went on tiptoe, pulling at his head to draw him down to her. He slammed his mouth across hers with a bruising need, and she parted her lips. Hot, slippery sweeps of his tongue ignited her, and she couldn't get close enough.

Lifting her, he nudged the truck door shut and turned for the house. Kissing her all the way across the yard to the small front porch. When he raised his head, she was gasping.

He gave her a quirk of a smile and let her slide down his body until her boots touched the floorboards. While he unlocked the front door—three locks, she noted—she tried to still the pounding of her heart, to no avail. It thundered in her chest like a herd of bulls breaking free.

For a woman who lived by the code of being in control, the idea of submitting was far too exciting.

He pushed open the door and waved for her to enter first. She stepped into the space, registering very few furnishings. "It looks like you just moved in."

"Place was furnished when I moved in. Guess I haven't done much to the place since then." He raised a shoulder and let it fall. "I pay the rent check, keep the power turned on and sleep here most nights. That's all."

She looked up into his eyes. Aiden Roshannon was a hard man, but she hadn't thought of him being someone who didn't live outside of work. When he spoke of his childhood home Eagle Crest, his eyes lit up.

Curling his fingers into her long hair, he gazed deep into her eyes. "It'll take me a minute to get things ready for us. Do you want to watch some TV?"

She blinked. How could she ever sit still while he rigged up his bedroom with whatever he would use to dominate her? She shook her head. "Could I... watch you?"

He gave a small nod. Then he reached out and twisted the three locks on the door, closing them in. "C'mon."

The thumps of his boots on the wooden floors sent chills up her back as she followed him into what might have been used as a dining room but was Aiden's storage space and depository. Everything from boxes to a coffee table with a broken leg sat there.

He threw her an apologetic look. "This is all stuff I need to get around to putting away. I admit, I'm not a great housekeeper."

Somehow, his words endeared him to her a little more. Everything about his life screamed that he was lonely, though a stubborn man like him would never admit to it.

"Maybe I'll come by and help you sometime."

He searched her face as if seeking a lie but then nodded. "That'd be nice. I could grill ya a nice thick steak." He straightened, pulling a length of rope from a box he'd been digging through. "And then fuck you until you don't know your own name."

* * * * *

Amaryllis's breath whooshed from her, and she planted a hand on the wall as if to hold herself up. He wasn't in much better shape—jittery as a cat in a cowboy dance hall, his body tense with arousal and worry about what was to come.

If things went bad between them, working conditions would be unbearable. If he scared her or hurt her, he'd never forgive himself.

There was still time for him to back off, to just have normal vanilla sex, maybe push her with a few commands. But deep down, he knew that would never be enough when it came to Amaryllis. The need to claim her was too strong. His mind too fogged with it.

222

Besides the rope, he grabbed a small black box that was locked with a padlock. He tucked it under his arm and tilted his head toward the hall leading to his room. "Ladies first."

She made a faint noise and started toward his room. Her strawberry blonde hair swaying on her back, her round ass inviting more lustful thoughts than ever. His dick throbbed.

After they entered his room, Amaryllis turned to him, her expression guarded.

"This is a little out of my territory," he said quietly, setting down the rope and box. "I've never started with a woman standing here watching me."

"Do you want me to go?"

"It's not that. I just worry I'll scare you off."

She glanced down at her hands and then back up at his face. "I'd like to see, if that's okay."

She'd take what control she could get. He understood that.

With her looking so worried, nibbling her bottom lip, he couldn't ignore her and start stringing ropes from his bedposts.

He reached for her. Drawing her close, wrapping his arms around her curvy body and breathing in her sweet scents. "I feel something different with you, Amaryllis."

"Me too," she breathed against his shoulder.

He cupped the back of her head and held her. "Let's explore it then. If you trust me."

She drew back enough to meet his gaze. "I do."

"Good." He stepped away and grabbed the rope. Though he hadn't done this in a long time, creating the wrist and ankle restraints was like second nature. Four loops of rope that could be tightened around her limbs hung from the four corners of his bed. Then he was left with one long length of rope coiled on the bedcovers.

The hemp called to him, begged for his fingers to work the knots that would secure Amaryllis's beautiful body for him. His cock was so stiff, and if he didn't release it from his jeans soon, he'd be in more pain.

But he had to take this slow. So fucking slow, turn her on so fucking much that she was dripping wet and begging him.

"Take off your clothes."

A breath escaped her parted lips. She only hesitated a second before bending over and removing her boots. As each piece of clothing created a pile on the floor, he watched. All the while, the locked black box seemed to scream for him to open it, to find his whip, light flogger, paddle.

Having those grips in his hands again…

And with this woman…

He swallowed hard, feeling his Adam's apple bulge against his throat.

When she peeled off her jeans, revealing silky black panties, he couldn't bite back his groan. Her gaze snapped to his.

"So fucking beautiful," he murmured.

That flush he was beginning to live for climbed her breasts and throat to settle in her cheeks. She sent him coy glances as she removed her bra. Her breasts bounced free, ripe, the tips already distended in invitation for his tongue.

"Cup them together. Hold them up for me."

A shudder ran through her as she curled her fingers around the bottoms of each breast, pushing them up and together. He stepped up to her and tossed his hat aside. Dipping his head, he snaked his tongue around one areola and then the other. Lapping each until it swelled more for him. Then swirling his tongue around and around. When small noises started escaping her lips, he sent her a piercing look.

And clamped her nipples between his fingers. Hard enough to sting, to let her feel the bite of what he could give her, the juxtaposition of pleasure and pain. How the pain mixed itself up and heightened the need.

She cried out.

"Don't look away from me."

She centered on him again as he applied pressure to her sensitive nipples.

"If I get some clamps for you, will you wear them?"

She bit into her lower lip again as if to trap another cry and nodded.

With a rumble of pleasure, he released her nipples. Then he leaned in to bathe them with his tongue again. She made a strangled noise and cupped his head to her.

Fuck, she was reacting the way he wanted, needed, craved. After sucking each for long minutes, he reached around her and clamped a hand on her ass cheek. Hard enough to draw another cry from her.

"On the bed, face down. Arms up and legs spread."

"Oh God, Aiden." Her voice shivered.

He looked deep into her eyes. "I'll take care of you. Give you everything you need. Trust me."

"I do," she whispered.

He nodded and gave her a little nudge toward the bed. She climbed onto it, giving him a perfect view of her backside. Tiny panties cut upward on her cheeks, revealing the curves and highlighting the space between her thighs. He bit his inner cheek to hold back the growl of want bulging at his throat.

She stretched her hands toward the bedposts and spread her thighs.

"Farther."

She obeyed.

"Fuck." Her panties rode up more, and the lips of her pussy against the fabric made him want to pull out his cock and pound her hard and fast until she was screaming for him.

He gripped his cock and squeezed. Counted to ten. When he had more control, he stepped to the front of the bed and looped her wrists in the ropes. He slid the knots until she was secure and tested that they weren't too tight.

"If your hands go numb or tingle at any point, tell me and I'll stop."

She nodded, her eyes hazy with a passion that only fueled his fires.

He moved around to her feet and repeated his movements. When she was stretched across his bed, he took one look at her ass and could barely see straight. He went for the black box.

The combination wasn't hard to remember — his birthday. When he opened the lid and saw the paddle nestled in the black velvet alongside the coiled whip, some of the tension went out of him.

This was right.

This was him and Amaryllis. Together they'd explore and draw closer. Deep down, he knew once he had what he wanted from her that he'd never give her up.

That should scare the hell out of a man like him — ex-Marine, war-hardened with a career in the law. Hell, he didn't keep a dog around because he couldn't invest the time in one. But Amaryllis was different.

He removed his shirt and let it drop to the floor. The clink of his belt buckle had Amaryllis turning her head to see. Good — she was growing aware of sounds, letting them heighten her desire.

She moved restlessly against the mattress as he unzipped his jeans slow inch by slow inch.

"No rubbing your pussy on the bed. That's mine."

She stilled but her breaths came out harsher.

With his clothes off, his cock stood straight up on his abs, purple and ready. He reached into the box and pulled out a cock ring. The small nubby fingers encircling his dick felt like fucking heaven and hell in one little circlet.

"Flex your hands for me."

She did, showing him that she had good feeling.

"Feet too."

She wiggled her ankles and toes.

"Good girl." He took the paddle from the velvet and closed the lid.

Her back bowed at attention.

"I'm going to spank your ass, Amaryllis. I'm going to show you that I'm in charge and you will take every smack with a thank-you, Master. Do you hear me?"

She nodded.

"Say it for me."

"Thank you... M-Master."

Fuck. He dropped his head forward, power and joy rushing through his veins. Three deep breaths and five heartbeats later, he began.

* * * * *

Amaryllis's nerves felt like they'd been draped over an electric fence. A thousand watts of need blasted her system as Aiden brought what felt like a paddle down on her ass cheek.

The hard smack sent her reeling, her breath gushing from her lungs.

And her clit swelling.

He made a guttural noise. "Again."

"Thank you, Master."

"Face forward, sub. Push your ass up."

Oh God, her panties were soaking, her pussy aching for his fingers, lips, cock. Who knew this lawman from small-town Wyoming was a Dom with all the skills to light her on fire? He must have gotten involved in some kinky shit in the service.

Another *crack* had her stiffening. The sting blasted through her panties and into her skin. She cried out and was rewarded with a brush of his fingers over the spot he'd just spanked.

She clung to that softness. If he'd give her more of that, she could endure a hundred more swats.

Well, maybe not that many.

"What do you say, sub?"

Her mind caught up. "Thank you, Master."

He made a contented noise. "You don't listen to me in the field and that's okay. You do your job and you're damn good at it,

Amaryllis. But in this room, I am your Master and you will listen to everything I say."

She nodded. Panting hard. She needed another spank. Oh God, had she just thought that? What had she turned into?

A third smack had her rising onto her knees, pushing back. "Thank you, Master," she said on a moan.

"Jesus God," he groaned.

Did that mean he liked her reaction?

Another spank came down harder on the other cheek. Three for each and her bottom was beginning to feel swollen. Even through her panties, she knew her cheeks were red and warm. Between her thighs, her clit pulsated to the rhythm of his paddle.

He delivered several more swats to each cheek and then stopped. Her heart seemed too loud in the silence—could he hear it?

She dragged in a shuddering breath. "Master?"

"Yes, sub."

"I need your touch."

As if he'd been waiting to hear just that, he let out a hasty breath. Something wooden— probably the paddle—hit the floor. When he touched her, she expected to feel his wide palms and long, rough fingers, and was shocked by his lips.

Soft kisses roaming over her cheeks, spattered down to the undercurve of her ass and back up. She shook with desire. If this was what giving herself up to Aiden meant, then she'd made the best decision of her life. Her mind was blanked to any worries. Cattle rustlers, ranchers, her brothers and the prospect of owning her own small farm all fled her mind.

She lived right here, right now in this room with Aiden.

He slipped his tongue under the elastic edge of her panties. The warm wetness spread up to the place where he'd spanked her left cheek. He walked his fingers up her inner thighs, and she tugged her bonds so hard that the bedframe rattled.

He chuckled and continued to torment her, almost skimming his fingers over her needy pussy but backing off enough to drive her crazy.

"Please. Touch me."

"When I say you're ready."

She wanted to put her arms around his neck and draw him down for a deep kiss. To feel his strength wrapped around her. Passion rose up and consumed her. She wasn't going to walk away from this experience the same person. She had changed since meeting Aiden.

In a very short time, she had found something she hadn't known she wanted.

Needed.

He hooked his fingers in her panties and yanked them down. A beat of silence followed but she felt his gaze on her backside.

"Cherry red for me. Your skin's so easily marked. I knew it."

"It's the red hair in me."

He spanned his hands across her bum, letting her feel where the edges of the paddle had marked her. Her skin felt fiery hot and she was so turned on.

His hands left her, and he got off the bed. The mattress dipped under her. What was next on this roller-coaster journey into the unknown?

The rough bite of hemp around her middle made her gasp. She pushed to her knees again, twisting to try to see him. Not seeing what he was doing only made her more aware of her vulnerability, but it filled her with sudden calm.

She went still.

"Good sub. I'm going to tie this rope around you and suspend you."

"Oh God." How would that even work? She was no dainty flower. She was muscular and curvy. Would ropes support her weight without cutting her in pieces?

She had to trust him.

He worked the rope around and around her, up to her ribs and down to her hips, creating a net. Then he strung the first corner to the bedpost. She felt her upper body rise off the bed.

"This shouldn't hurt. If it cuts into your skin at all, you say the word and I'll stop."

Oklahoma was her safe word. But she was fine—better than fine. She was fucking fantastic and ready for more.

"Yes, Aiden."

"Master," he corrected in that deep voice that was like the river flowing over rocks.

Somewhere on the floor, her phone tinkled a ring tone. Aiden stopped and turned from the bed. She heard a plastic sound as he set her phone back down. Whoever had called was definitely not reaching her tonight.

When Aiden worked her other side off the bed, he was slightly rougher. Could he be feeling the same desperate need she was? When they finally came together, neither would be able to hold back and she knew part of him wanting her this way was to pull that out of her.

With her upper body suspended off the mattress, she waited. He couldn't work quickly enough.

* * * * *

Aiden didn't want to see that fucking name flash across Amaryllis's phone screen. JD. Who the fuck was he?

Aiden kept telling himself that she was here with him, wearing his ropes, his red paddle marks and soaking wet for him. Yet some other man was calling her.

He freed her legs long enough to remove her panties and then winched her off the bed completely. She hung there, inches from the mattress. Her belly dipped lower, and he didn't want her back to suffer for it, so he found a pillow and eased it beneath her. That would help stabilize her for when he fucked her too.

"All right, sub?" His quiet question sounded harsh.

"Aiden. Master. I need to see you. Please." Her words were choppy and his heart contracted at the sound of her uncertainty. She was asking for a connection, and he could not deny her.

He walked to the head of the bed and knelt to look into her eyes. One glance and he was a

235

goner, thoughts of JD fled. He leaned in and kissed her forehead, her cheeks, her lips. She turned her face up for his kiss.

When he raised his head, his throat was tight, aching with emotion. She was knotting him up as much as he had her with his ropes.

She issued a shaky breath. "I want you so bad I can't think."

Her admission sent him into full Dom mode. He stood. Knotted her hair in his fist and guided his cock toward her mouth. He skimmed it across her lips, back and forth. She opened for him, but he resisted sinking into her sweet heat. Two pumps and he'd be a goner.

Need exploded inside him, but somehow, he managed to draw back and move behind her.

The sight of her ass, hiked up, her cheeks reddened from his paddle, and the shadow of wet pussy between her thighs dragged a groan from him. He didn't hesitate—he crawled onto the bed and buried his face between her legs.

She cried out as he sank his tongue into her wet folds and thumbed her clit at the same time. The bed shook with her trembles—or were they his?

Her flavor coated his tongue, driving him to give her the best orgasm of her life.

It didn't take long. She started to contract around his tongue. He flicked faster, deeper. She issued a loud moan and then juices gushed over his lips as her release struck. Her circled her clit with his forefinger, extending her pleasure. When she started to pant and gasp, he raised his head.

* * * * *

She'd never seen a man in real life wear a cock ring, and it was fucking hot as hell. She'd ached to take his length into her throat and feel that ring against her lips, but he'd denied her. As he was so fond of doing.

Bastard, she thought with extreme affection.

Now he'd just given her an earth-shaking orgasm and wouldn't put his cock in her fast enough. She half expected him to paddle her some more, but that never came.

She didn't know if she was disappointed or not.

"Can you come with a cock ring?" she asked.

"Hell yeah. Makes it much more intense and lasts longer."

"Mmm."

"Curiosity satisfied, sub?"

"Yes. Aiden... Master. Fuck me."

"You want me to fuck you? Like this?" He thrust two fingers into her pussy, high and deep. She screamed as bliss washed over her like a tidal wave. With his digits in her snug depths, she lost all sense of reality and only felt.

He withdrew, dragging her wetness with his fingers, and then plunged back in.

"Oh God." Not feeling the bed beneath her, only the prickly ropes and the soft pillow, gave her a sense of floating. She was only anchored by his touch. Those two fingers working their magic in and out of her pussy.

"You're so fucking ready for me. You need my cock." He bit off the words.

"Yessss."

"You want me buried deep in you, splitting you with my thrusts."

"Oh God, yes. Please."

He speared her again, pressing a spot that made her flood with juices. He groaned. A second later, he pulled his fingers free and his cock entered her in one hard shove.

Filled completely, her mind, heart and soul all wrapped up in the moment along with her body, which was singing for more. He grasped her by the hips and burrowed into her. His hips slapped her body, the sound mingling with their combined groans.

She'd never been so consumed by a man or, well, by anything in her life. She closed her eyes and let Aiden have all of her. When she felt him stiffen, she knew he was close. Helplessly strung, she couldn't move to get what they both needed.

But he did that all by himself.

With a harsh grunt, he slammed into her, and her inner walls contracted with an orgasm so fierce it stole her breath. A rush of liquid heat bathed her insides as his own roared release shattered the air.

For long minutes, she floated on a haze of ecstasy. When he rocked his hips into her one last time, they shared a moan.

"You were right," she whispered.

"About what, doll?" So she was no longer sub. Their session was over. Now they were entangled in brand new ways.

"Good thing we didn't do that at the B&B."

Chapter Twelve

Aiden meticulously recorded all the findings of the past two days in his notebook. Each detail from their last trip to the slaughterhouse, where three of the cows wore ear tags that belonged to one of the ranchers with stolen cattle. That the animals had been returned to the owner, but God knew how many more had already been processed in the facility.

His mind kept returning to his night with Amaryllis. He'd made her come so many times. She'd worn his ropes like the beautiful sex goddess she was.

And he was fucking falling in love with her.

She also had more than one call from JD that night. Whoever the fucking guy was, he was persistent. As far as Aiden knew, she hadn't returned the calls while at his house. After a long night of passion, they'd showered together, finding release in each other's arms under the spray of water.

Then he'd taken her to the B&B for a set of clean clothes. She'd insisted on him leaving her there and driving herself back in that monster truck of hers while Aiden took the latest call on another slaughter. This time a calf.

He ground his molars back and forth as he stared at his notebook. Part of his case was in the county where Judd was sheriff, and without his twin's input, he felt he was missing too many pieces of the puzzle.

He picked up his cell and texted Amaryllis.

Where are you?

Crossroads.

You coming to the office?

He wanted to ask who JD was.

Be there in two.

He tapped his pen on his desk. He had to find out where her mind was. If she felt the same as he did — if she couldn't think or even see straight since their night together.

When he heard the rumble of the big diesel truck, he launched to his feet and strode outside. By the time she'd scaled her way to the ground, he stood in front of her.

"We're going to Eagle Crest."

Her eyes widened. "Right now?"

"Yes."

"What's there? What is happening?"

"Judd has a couple guys in his county that have dropped names and given information on

241

our case. We need to go talk to him." He didn't want to say that he needed to see how she acted around his brother and cousin, if Wes could even get there in time. He was down south on the trail of a criminal who'd broken bond.

What would his family think of Amaryllis? She was breathtaking, and that air of confidence was something all three Roshannon men admired in a female. But no way was he sharing with Wes like he had years ago. Amaryllis was his alone.

He looked into her warm brown eyes and wondered if he was making a mistake. Staking his claim by taking her home wasn't exactly a good idea, was it? Part of him hoped it would show him that his heart was on the right trail.

Minutes later, they were in his truck, each with an overnight bag. Amaryllis was focused on her phone, her thumbs working across the screen.

"Who're you texting?"

"Guy from the auction. He says he has surveillance video of something we need to see."

He swung his gaze to her. "Does that mean we're driving over there now?"

She nodded. "A short detour. I know you're eager to get home to Eagle Crest."

He drew his brows together. "Why do you say that?"

"I know you love your home. But I think you should make your place here in Crossroads feel more like a haven, a place where you can relax and unwind."

Directing his attention to the road again, he thought about what she said. During his years spent in the military, he didn't have much to call his own. Now that he could, he hadn't bothered. He didn't feel at home anywhere except Eagle Crest. But being there once a month wasn't enough.

Her phone rang, and she shot him a sideways glance before answering. "What's up, JD?'

Aiden's spine stiffened. She surely wouldn't take a call from a lover in Texas while in the truck with him — and after a night like they'd shared?

"Yeah, I got the information you sent. I haven't done anything about the mortgage yet. I'm feeling a little up in the air about the decision now."

Aiden fixed his attention at her.

"I'm not sure I want the responsibility of a farm. I'm more of a free spirit, on the road chasing criminals." She met Aiden's stare. Was it his imagination or was there something else in her eyes? Something unsaid?

While she finished her conversation, he pondered everything. Including why he was so damn upset that she was talking to another man and what that look she'd sent him was all about.

When she hung up, she leaned back in her seat with a sigh. "Why does family think they always know what's best for you?"

He jerked his head around. "Family?"

"Yeah, that was my brother, JD. He's been helping me with my idea about buying that small farm, and now that I've told him my misgivings, he pours it on thicker, saying I need something of my own, a home base, a place to raise a family, blah blah. What if I don't want those things?"

Aiden's heart had leaped into his throat at the word brother. It took him a full second to focus on the other things she'd said. "You just lectured me on having something of my own, but maybe the farm isn't for you. Do you want a family?"

"Well, sure. Someday. But I'm happy with my work and I don't think I can shimmy through windows with a big, pregnant belly."

"You shouldn't be shimmying through windows at all." Making her follow the rules was like asking a pig not to eat—impossible.

She made a face and he chuckled. Suddenly he sobered, a picture of her ripe with a child popping all too easily in his mind. "Amaryllis, we need to talk."

"What about?" Her voice held a note of hesitation.

"About us."

She twisted her fingers together. "What do you want to discuss?"

"Well, my family's going to ask plenty of questions, which I'm sure you can guess. We are work colleagues, firstly. But I want you to know that I'm feeling more for you."

Her gaze flew to his. He held it for a long second before glancing at the road again to keep from having an accident.

"I'm not sure how you feel," he said.

She tugged at a tendril of hair. "I'm not sure either. Been thinking about us a lot, especially since last night. What happened… it broke down some barriers in us and I feel like I learned more about you in one night than I could have dating a man for a year."

He nodded. "Domination has a way of doing that. The trust, the giving."

"It draws you closer," she whispered.

He nodded, his chest stuffed full of emotion he had no idea how to put into words. He gave a nod to cover the moment. "Seems we're on the same page then." Though neither had said much at all, he felt more at ease. He reached across the console and covered her hand with his, squeezing.

"We'll go to the auction to view that video and then on to Eagle Crest. I promise not to let my family scare you too much."

She chuckled. "Takes a hell of a lot to scare me, Roshannon. Besides, how can I possibly meet anybody more complicated than you?"

* * * * *

Turned out she'd spoken too soon. All three Roshannon men—four if you included their father—were as serious as the next. When she'd set eyes on Judd walking across the yard from the barn, she'd nearly had a heart attack, thinking Aiden had somehow cloned himself. Then when Wes pulled into the driveway and got out of his truck, she'd believed she was seeing in triple.

They all had the same wide shoulders and strong jaws. Wes was slightly taller and had spent some time bulking up his chest and arms, but other than that, there was no way the same blood didn't pulse through these men's veins.

246

"You can't be cousins. You have to be brothers," she said.

Wes and Judd exchanged a look but Aiden gave a nod. "We get that a lot. Amaryllis, meet my twin brother Judd and my cousin Wes."

Both men tipped their hats to her using a gesture that was so similar to Aiden's that it was eerie.

A male voice sounded from behind, a clearing of a throat. They all turned to see an older cowboy, hardened to steel from years in the saddle, his hair thick and white under his Stetson. In his face, she saw the lines mirrored more faintly in Aiden's and Judd's. Something about the stern expression in his eyes reminded her more of Aiden, though.

"You must be Aiden's father." She extended a hand.

"Boone Roshannon. I've read a lot about you, Ms. Long."

"Amaryllis." She smiled. Not exactly at ease with the group—she'd never met the family of someone she was romantically involved with before. But being on her turf—grazing land, cattle and barns—gave her a bit more confidence.

"Glad to have you here, Amaryllis. Make yourself at home. I need these boys for a little chore."

They trio went on high alert. Boone clapped Aiden on the back, since he was nearest. "We've got three-hundred head to move. All hands on deck."

"I can ride," Amaryllis said.

Aiden met her stare. A flutter in her belly began. She knew that look, had seen it the previous night so many times while he was in control. The blazing expression was seared into her memory. When she returned to Texas, at least she'd have something to replay on the chilly nights alone.

She grabbed his forearm and towed him several feet away. "Can I speak with you?"

Behind them, his family chuckled.

"You're not going, Amaryllis. I'll let you saddle up and watch, but you're not getting into the thick of those steers."

She rolled her eyes. "What do you think I grew up doing? Playing Barbie dolls? I've been running cattle since I was twelve."

"Not this time." His look said this was one of those times he wanted control outside the bedroom.

She cocked her head. "What do I get out of it if I stay behind?"

He stepped up to her, body heat scorching her front. Curling his fingers around her upper arms, he hovered his lips a scant inch from hers. "You get my cock deep in your pussy and my palm on your ass while you beg for more."

His low-pitched voice sent rivers of need through her body to pool in her belly. When he leaned in and stamped her mouth with a kiss that was hard and yet held so much meaning, her mind spun.

Before she could regain her wits, he turned and strode back to the guys. "Let's do this."

Wes nudged him in the shoulder and received a playful punch in return. Judd hung back to walk with Amaryllis, which confused her if she didn't consciously consider who he was. Having a man beside her who was so like Aiden gave her the urge to grab his hand.

The way he'd just kissed her in front of them meant their connection was out in the open. He *had* admitted to feeling more. And so had she, which had really surprised her. Things were moving fast between them.

"You're legendary in the South," Judd said.

She shot him a smile. "Thanks, but I just do my job."

"A damn fine one, from what I hear. You keeping my rigid-ass brother on his toes?" He sent her the same gray-eyed stare that Aiden gave, the one that had been haunting her since the first day they'd met.

She swallowed her giggle. Aiden really was rigid—did that mean Judd was the opposite? She'd heard about twins who swung opposite in personalities. "We're working fine together."

He arched a brow that said that kiss they'd shared hadn't gone unnoticed. "This crime ring is stretching far and wide. Whether or not some of the crimes are related is still to be determined, but I think plenty are."

She nodded. "We believe the butcherings and the thefts are connected, but we haven't put two and two together yet."

"At dinner, maybe we can all sit down and talk business."

She pressed her lips together. She wasn't in a habit of airing secrets of her work over the evening meal, but the Roshannons were all lawmen. And she supposed their daddy was as close-lipped as the rest of them. She hadn't met their momma yet, but she imagined the woman knew the implications of leaking gossip.

Amaryllis nodded. "We'll have to get Aiden to take out his notebook."

Judd tossed back his head and released a low, hearty chuckle. "He still carries that thing?"

Ahead of them, Aiden and Wes twisted to see what was going on. Aiden's brows drew together.

"Uh-oh. Now he's gonna walk back and give me hell. I'll speak with you later. Gotta get saddled up." Judd broke into a jog as Aiden did exactly what he'd guessed.

"What was that about?" Aiden asked.

"We were talking about your notebook."

His ears reddened and his steely eyes softened. "Judd's always been an ass. C'mon, let's get you a horse."

Surprised by this new, lighter, more easy-going Aiden, she quickened her pace to follow him to the barn. Watching him joke around with his brother and Wes made her realize that he really was different here — at home. When some of the ranch hands gathered, already on horseback, Aiden greeted each with affection.

After Aiden selected a solid mare that was easy to handle for her, she slipped into the saddle. "God, I missed this. I haven't ridden in too long."

"Me either. Maybe I need a place of my own with a couple horses." His eyes twinkled at the idea.

"I was thinking the same thing."

Their gazes connected for such a long moment that she felt the need to look away but couldn't. Right now, their link was so strong that she practically felt him holding the end of a rope that was bound around her. Earlier when her brother had called, she hadn't had an inkling of what her dreams were. Now, after a few minutes on Eagle Crest, she knew.

She wanted to see Aiden smile more.

Riding with a group gave her another sort of thrill. The breeze on her skin, the fall of hooves on the turf. Eagle Crest was a well-kept ranch nestled between mountains that rose up smoky blue against the paler blue sky. She dragged in a deep breath of horse and grasses crushed under hoof.

After a ten-minute ride, they came upon the herd. "Is that what we're moving?" she asked Aiden, who rose close to her.

"That's what *we're* moving. You're going to hang back."

She sighed. "Normally I'd fight you tooth and nail for my place in this, but it's your ranch."

He blinked at her like an owl.

"What?"

"You actually backed down. I can't believe you didn't kick your horse into a run, circle the cattle and do it all yourself."

She stared straight ahead at the hats of men bobbing with the rise and fall of their horses and beyond that, the dark blot of cattle. "There's still time. Don't tempt me."

He chuckled and reached over to squeeze her shoulder.

A whistle sounded, and Aiden perked up. "That's me. Promise me you'll hang back."

Since it was so important to him and it didn't bother her to watch so many strong men at work, she nodded.

The men began to close around the herd in a semi-circle as a barrier. Then two riders rode the inside perimeter between horsemen and cattle, pushing the beasts in the direction they wanted them to go. When a cow would try to break loose, one of the border patrol would direct it back.

Amaryllis reined up to watch their progress, which didn't seem to take long considering the amount of wayward cattle. She kept her gaze on Aiden's hat, though sometimes she lost it among the sea of ranch hands. He and Judd worked together well, anticipating the other's moves, working closely yet staying out of each other's way.

Another loud whistle, and the entire group of riders moved forward, funneling the cattle toward a road.

She edged up close, fixated on the rider who went ahead up the road to block any traffic for the herd. She hadn't been told what they were doing, but by her guess, there was another pasture down the road that could be reached most easily this way.

The air was filled with moos and a dog up near Aiden that kept nipping at one wayward cow's legs to keep it in line. Broad backs of cowboys moved ahead of her, bringing up the rear of the herd.

She felt slightly sweaty, taking it all in. The testosterone, the beauty of the sight. Her pulse was hammering, and she realized she'd gotten bitten by the ranching bug all over again. She hadn't felt this way since her teen years. Now when she returned to her family ranch, her brother, Ulyss, was such a rigid dictator that she didn't stick around long. But this reminded her how it was to work as a team toward one big goal.

She pressed her heels into her horse and guided it forward, riding at the rear, her heart lifted.

* * * * *

After Amaryllis met his momma and was shown to the bathroom to wash up for dinner, Aiden paced the hall waiting for her.

"She's not going to escape, bro," Wes said as he spotted Aiden.

"You don't know Amaryllis. She can shimmy out a window lickety-split."

Wes cocked a brow. "Interesting talent. May be useful."

"Yeah, plenty useful." Though he still hadn't forgotten the way his heart had pounded when she'd launched into that abandoned grocery.

"She's handy to have around then." Wes pushed the conversation.

Aiden turned to him. Squared his shoulders. "Look, I know what you're doing."

Wes chuckled. "What's that?"

"Trying to edge in. We aren't eighteen anymore, and she isn't Lorna."

Wes swung his gaze to the closed bathroom door several feet down the hallway. "Sure about that?"

"No." Aiden's voice came out as a low growl. "She isn't because I'm not willin' to share. So back off."

Wes held his glare a moment and then chuckled. "Been waitin' for you to come back to us."

Confusion made Aiden's brows pinch. "What's that supposed to mean? I come here as often as I can, same as you."

Wes shook his head, his slightly shaggy hair falling into his eyes. "I mean that you were here in body but not in spirit. Not since you left for the Marines."

And definitely not since he'd come home for good. Aiden swallowed hard. The notion that, somehow, the missing pieces of himself had found their way home and made him whole again seemed right on.

The door opened, and Aiden spun to Amaryllis. She froze, looking nervous. "I'm sorry, were you guys waiting for the bathroom? Sorry it took a bit. I was grubbier than I thought and the water's really hot."

"Just waiting on you." Aiden stepped forward, the need to put his hands on her a burning ember in his chest.

Wes said, "I'll see if your momma needs any help gettin' dinner on the table."

When he'd left Aiden and Amaryllis alone, Aiden said, "He always was a suck-up, settin' the table every meal and making me and Judd look lazy as dogs in a puddle of sunshine."

She looked up at him. "What is the tension I feel in you, really?"

"It's nothing. Let's go see if Judd's around."

Turned out Judd was outside with the ranch hands and had to be called to the table by their annoyed mother. But once they were all seated, she beamed at them. "I love having my boys around me. And Amaryllis, we're so happy you're here."

Under the table, Aiden squeezed her thigh. She clenched her muscle and smiled at him and then his momma. "Thank you for having me, and on short notice."

"Always plenty to go around. Now tell us all about your case." His momma picked up a serving spoon and took a helping of noodles swimming in gravy.

Amaryllis made a surprised sound in her throat but quickly swallowed it. "Um, maybe Aiden can start it off."

He shot her a crooked smile. Seeing Amaryllis out of her element was giving him a new glimpse of her. He liked this softer version of her as much as he loved the badass who would tackle grown men and dig a knee into their backs.

Food was passed, the details of the case discussed. Judd interjected with a few bits about what was going on in his county, and Wes contributed a name of a solid lead for them to check out later.

Amaryllis glanced up at Aiden. "Aren't you gonna put that in your notebook?"

Everyone at the table laughed, including his parents. Aiden sent her a look that said, *I'll get you alone sooner or later.* She squirmed in her seat, satisfying him on another level.

"There's got to be one person who started this off. They didn't hold a meetin' down at the grange hall looking for members of an illegal cattle theft ring," Wes said.

Aiden forked a bite of roast beef and waved it over his plate as he spoke. "Amaryllis and I have discussed that. Who and the motive behind it."

"That's easy," Judd said around his own bite of beef, "money. Man doesn't get power or prestige from stealing cattle."

"No, but he sure must have made it look enticing to his buddies to get so many in on it."

"I've seen that in the South plenty." When Amaryllis spoke, everyone listened. "I've actually brought two bands of rustlers down that had one very influential ringleader each."

"How'd you do it?" Judd asked. "What were your tactics?"

She shot Aiden a look. "I don't think you want to know."

Aiden chuckled. "Amaryllis doesn't always do things by the book."

"Which is why Latchaw brought her up here, right? He didn't care about the hows but wanted it to end fast."

"I already feel like we've been working the case forever and don't have nearly enough leads." Amaryllis set aside her fork, nibbling her lower lip. Aiden squeezed her thigh again. She was kicking herself for not running out, identifying her criminal immediately and hauling him in, tied up in a neat little package, within five minutes of being in Wyoming.

"It's a big crime. A lot going on. There's no way to solve it quickly. But we need to follow the leads we have from Wes and Judd. There's also that slaughterhouse video tape."

"What was on it?" Judd asked.

Wes's gaze was steady on Amaryllis, and Aiden caught his stare with cocked brow of challenge.

"Oh hell, here we go again." Judd sat back in his seat.

Everyone at the table tensed. Amaryllis looked between them. "What's going on?" she asked.

"Nothing," he and Wes said at the same time.

Judd chuckled. "These two have tastes that run the same in women. Back when we were eighteen—"

"Enough, Judd," their momma said with a flush of horror crawling over her face.

Aiden felt the metal of the fork in his hand flex he was gripping it so hard. He shook his head. "We're talking the job here and you bring that shit up, Judd?"

"I didn't bring it up. Just made an observation is all. Now about that surveillance tape."

Amaryllis was confused but she sure wouldn't be for long. A woman like her would have questions, demand answers. By the end of the evening, Aiden would have aired all his dirty laundry and given details about the time he and Wes had shared a young woman.

Aiden wasn't sure how he felt about telling the tale, especially when he didn't know how she'd react. He didn't want her to think he was willing to share her with anybody.

"Amaryllis, do you want to tell them about the video?" he asked quietly.

She nodded. "They caught a man driving up in a gray pickup with a trailer on. He spoke with someone in the slaughterhouse, who led him inside. Money changed hands, they shook on trust, the cows were unloaded and ten minutes later they were on the processing line. Aiden and I believe a few were from the group stolen from Owens."

Judd scratched his jaw. "Now that sounds interesting, doesn't it? When were those cows stolen?"

"Beginning of the week."

"So this rustler's got a place to hold several cows while he sells them off in different places. Who was the guy? Did you get a look at his face? A name?"

"Got the face first. The name later."

"Explain," Wes said, his attention more on the talk than on Amaryllis, which made Aiden breathe easier.

"Amaryllis had the idea to call around to stores that sell pricey items, like electronics or off-road vehicles. She asked if anybody had made any big purchases lately that seemed unusual or stuck out in the owners' minds. Then she got a description."

"And it matches the guy in the video." Judd crossed his arms over his chest, his meal forgotten as often happened when they talked cases. Even as a kid, he couldn't think and eat at the same time.

Amaryllis and Aiden nodded.

"Is there a name connected to the face?" Wes asked.

"The guy paid in cash. But a man thought he recognized him. Right now, Latchaw has Hoyt on it, running records and investigating whereabouts."

"Who is it?" Judd asked.

"The guy came from Kansas a few months back, took a room at the B&B for a while before moving in with one of the waitresses down at Delaney's." Amaryllis looked between the people at the table, who waited for the name. "It's Owens' own nephew, Billy."

* * * * *

Amaryllis had been caught up in coming to Eagle Crest and meeting the Roshannons, but now that she was talking cases again, she was eager to get back on the road. She didn't like leaving things in the hands of other people, no matter how capable they were.

Aiden watched her pace the room they'd been given to share. Night had fallen, drawn around the ranch like a private velvet curtain closing them off from the world. He'd taken off his hat but hadn't moved to remove his boots yet. He just sat on the edge of the bed watching her like a big cat watched an antelope.

When she revolved past him again, he snagged her around the waist and pulled her down across his knees, dangling facedown. She cried out in surprise and jerked her head around to glare at him.

"What's that for?"

"Only way I can shut off your mind is when your ass is under my palm. The case can wait, Amaryllis. But we're alone right now."

"I've never worked anything this big," she protested. "It's exciting. I want to—"

Without warning, he brought the flat of his hand down on her ass. She broke off midsentence and hissed as the sting rang through her body.

Her nipples went from slightly pinched with arousal to full hardness in a blink and a throb took up residence between her legs.

"Now," he caressed her ass cheek through her jeans, "do I need to swat you again or are you ready to settle down for bed?"

She panted. "What case?"

His deep chuckle spread over her, warming her from the inside out. "Good little sub. Now stand up here and undress for me."

Several heartbeats passed before she could make her legs do her bidding and hold her weight. She stood before Aiden and reached for her shirt buttons. As she worked down the line of buttons, his eyelids drooped over his smoldering stare. She dipped a glance at his groin and found the crotch of his jeans bulging. This submission thing came with a power of its own, and she was seriously tripping on it.

Heart speeding faster, she removed her shirt and then her bra. Her boots and jeans followed, but she hesitated at her panties. Last time he'd wanted them on.

"Aiden?"

"Master," he corrected.

A shudder zipped through her. "Master. Do you want me to take them off?"

"Yes." The grittiness of his voice told her that he may not have all the control he liked tonight.

She hooked her thumbs in the sides of her panties and stopped. He caught her stare and held it prisoner.

"What is it?" he asked.

"What Judd said about you and Wes having the same taste in women. Was that what was going on in the hall while I was washing up for dinner?"

His jaw shifted as if he ground his teeth, and a muscle flickered in the crease. His five o'clock shadow looked like a bruise in the long shadows in the room.

"I don't like to talk about it, let alone when I have a naked woman standing in front of me. But you need to hear it before my idiot brother tells you."

She tried to even out her breathing. "Tell me."

"Back when we were eighteen, I started seeing this girl and turned out she was seeing Wes too. He got this idea we could just share her."

Amaryllis's eyebrows shot up. "You shared a woman with your cousin?"

"Neither of us was serious about her. We were young and full of cum. It didn't seem like a big deal. Wouldn't be now except Wes had his eye on you and well, that isn't happening." His tone sounded like *over my dead body*.

Or Wes's.

She let go of the breath she'd been holding. "Did you share her..."

He seemed to understand the question she couldn't put into words. "Not at the same time. Passed her between us mostly, but a few times we were all in the same room. Took turns."

Her nipples tightened at the sexual kinks her lover had experienced.

"Does it turn you on, the thought of being shared?" He looked up at her from where he still sat on the bed, a guarded expression on his face but his eyes holding a vulnerability she'd never seen before in Aiden or any other Roshannon.

She stepped up to stand between his knees. She wrapped her arms around his neck and brought his head to rest against her belly. "No.

265

It turns me on that my lover has enough experience to pleasure me the way I need it."

A sound broke from him, and he rubbed his stubbled jaw over her belly. Goosebumps rippled over her skin, down to her thighs. With his hands, he stroked her skin in long passes, from waist to knees and back up again. When he cupped her breasts, she swayed backward to give him complete access.

Then he pulled her down, pressing her under him as he claimed her mouth in a deep, sucking kiss. Warmth soon turned into a burning inferno. She wrapped her thighs around his hips, and he rocked his bulging cock into her bare pussy. The rough denim on her folds made her gasp, so he did it again.

And again.

Need spread through her so fast that she wasn't prepared for the blinding orgasm that struck. A groan escaped him, and he captured her nipple in his mouth, sucking as waves of release pounded her.

"Aiden…"

"Master."

"Master, you make me feel so good. I want you."

In a blink, he was on his feet, stripping off all his clothes and approaching the bed again in his full, naked, muscled glory. She saw the

Marine inside the velvet steel of his flesh and the Dom in the proud way his cock jutted against his six-pack abs. But in his eyes, she saw Aiden the man. The way he looked at her was almost as if…he loved her.

She opened her arms to him and he came into her with one smooth glide. Fucking her with a slow insistence that drown out the memory of any other man she'd ever had before him. Aiden pinned her wrists in one of his hands above her head, hovering over her in a one-armed pushup that turned her on as much as his rigid cock gliding in and out of her.

Drawing him closer with her thighs around his waist, she kissed him. The tangling of their tongues, the movements of their bodies, it was erotic as hell. And it meant so much more.

On instinct, she bit into his lower lip. He jerked back to look into her eyes. With a growl only a true alpha male could make, he began to pound into her. Claiming her.

* * * * *

He'd started out with control. Held onto the precious fibers of it. Until that love bite. She'd broken the skin on his lip, the little hellcat, and she'd pay for it as soon as he got his mind back.

Pleasure drove him deeper and deeper, his balls slapping her ass. As soon as he found his control again, he'd take that length of rope from under his bed and tie her up, ass in the air for his spanking.

But three thrusts turned into four. Pretty soon he couldn't stop. His mind blanked to anything but the hormones coursing through his veins and her sweet whimpers. He kissed them off her lips but soon he was silencing her cries with a hand over her mouth.

Her eyes were hazed, her body clenching and releasing in a rhythm that sent him over the edge far too soon.

He came hard with convulsive jerks of his hips as she tensed and squeezed around his cock, finding her own release.

Seconds passed as he tried to see straight again, and she bit his palm.

With a laugh, he removed his hand from her mouth and rolled, taking her with him. Tucking her close, smoothing his hands up and down her spine, still damp with the dew of their coupling.

Fatigue was catching up to him, and holding her this way only made him feel lazier. Her breathing changed, grew slower. Having her here in his old bed at Eagle Crest felt so fucking right. *Everything* about her felt fucking right.

"I'm not sharing you," he murmured against her hair.

Or letting you go back to Texas.

Chapter Thirteen

Amaryllis looked around her rented room in the B&B. She was lost, out of sorts, feeling like a weary traveler for the first time... well, ever.

Being at Eagle Crest had reminded her how it felt to be connected to something, part of a bigger whole. That feeling of loss had probably driven her to apply for the loan to buy the small farm weeks ago. But even if she got it, some of the most beautiful, rich land she'd ever seen, she'd be alone on it.

She tidied up the space, throwing all her laundry into a net bag. Today needed to be a laundry day, and she was almost looking forward to a mundane task. Since arriving in Crossroads, she practically hadn't sat down.

This case was definitely one of the biggest ones she'd ever dealt with. The people involved seemed to number in the range of a dozen. Cattle were stolen, taken to auctions in other counties, and hell, probably across state lines. Or they were being butchered for the cash. She turned these ideas over and over in her head and tried to attach the crimes to the names they knew and of those they'd arrested.

After she had her room organized and the bag of laundry ready, she headed out. It was the Lord's day and she hoped a small town like Crossroads had a coin laundry open on Sunday. She supposed she could ask the B&B owner to use the facility's machines, but she needed to get out for a while.

She opened the monster truck door and tossed the laundry up and in. As she settled behind the wheel, she giggled to think of Aiden's view on her driving this truck. She had a feeling if she drove up to his place and asked him to test-drive the bed, he'd leap in and like the roominess well enough.

Maybe she'd do just that. He seemed to prefer sex in a bed where he could control the environment right down to how much noise she made. But a romp in an unexpected place always made for a fun time.

The truck alerted her that she was low on fuel, so she headed toward the main strip of Crossroads and the mini-mart. Seeing the storefront made her think of flirting with Aiden over a chili dog.

Damn, she was worse off than she thought.

Aiden consumed her mind and ruled her body. It wasn't a good idea to let herself fall for him—she was going back to Texas after they made their arrests.

And it could be too late. She didn't want to leave Aiden, and surely that meant emotions were stirred up.

She pulled up to a diesel pump, cut the engine and then hopped out. A couple other cars were getting gas and someone was parked next to the building, probably grabbing one of those chili dogs.

As she reached high to connect the pump with the diesel tank opening, her mind roamed back to Aiden. Of seeing him with his family, smiling and carefree. At least when he wasn't posturing over Wes looking her direction. Luckily, Wes hadn't pushed and Aiden had gone back to his easier self after dinner.

There didn't seem to be any tension or hard feelings, and she was relieved. She didn't want to be the cause of a family argument.

She glanced up from the numbers flicking by on the pump screen, catching sight of a familiar back. She peered harder as the cowboy turned. That profile, the sharp nose and the way he wore his hat dipped low…

She ripped the nozzle from the truck and shoved the gas cap on. Striding across the parking lot fast to reach the guy before he jumped in the car and she lost sight of him.

Billy Owens.

"Hey! Can I talk to you for a second?" she called.

He shot her a glance, recognition spreading across his face rapid-fire. He yanked open the door of his car and leaped in. She didn't wait to see if he stopped—he wasn't going to.

She ran to her truck and had it on the road, speeding after him down the highway. She had their guy, the man who was probably responsible for most of the thefts and killings around here, heading the operation.

She thought of her cell phone in her back pocket and calling Aiden or the sheriff's office, but Sundays were lazy, and she didn't know if the secretary would even be there to answer a call.

Just then Owens made a wild right turn onto a gravel road that sent his car fishtailing. Amaryllis didn't hesitate. She knew how to drive big trucks and back roads were her Indy 500 track. She stomped on the gas. He didn't slow, just zoomed on in a cloud of dust.

She was higher than most of the dust Owens' car put off, luckily. If she could get close enough, she could pass and then use her truck as a blockade.

Her sidearm was in her handbag on the floor of the passenger's seat. Out of reach. She hoped she wouldn't need it. Going out to do laundry on a Sunday afternoon, she hadn't thought she needed to strap it to her thigh.

Her phone buzzed on her ass, and she lifted one cheek to pull it free. Her truck hit a patch of loose gravel and she spent a second biting her lip and skidding through it before she answered.

"Long."

"Amaryllis. What the fuck is going on? I just got a call from the mini-mart that they had a pump and run. Description of the truck matches that damn monster truck of yours Another call just came in about a truck speeding through a slow zone at a high speed."

"Aiden, don't give me any crap, okay? Yeah, it's me. I've got Owens in my sights and he's trying to race away."

A beat of silence had her wondering what the hell Aiden was thinking and not saying. The telling off she'd get would have to wait.

"Can't talk—I gotta stay alert."

"Don't hang up! What're your coordinates?"

She cast a wild look around the sides of the roads. Not a sign in sight. She didn't know these parts, and that was probably what Owens was counting on. He raced ahead of her, zigzagging as he took another turn at a high speed.

"We seem to be winding through the mountains. Twisty road, gravel. Headed west."

* * * * *

Aiden's blood ran cold. He stared at Latchaw.

Amaryllis was out there involved in a high-speed chase on one of the more treacherous roads leading out of Crossroads. He was too far away to give any help, and there was no way he'd catch them.

Latchaw stared back. The two of them had been having coffee in Delaney's when Latchaw had gotten a call about another ranch broken into, some farm implements stolen. On the heels of that was the call from the mini-mart and the speeding complaint.

Fuck, Amaryllis.

Could she even handle that monster truck on those roads?

He ripped off his hat and shoved his fingers through his hair.

"Let's get a read on her phone, find out her location." Latchaw grabbed his cell, nearly knocking over his coffee. They both stood and started outside.

On the way past the cash register, Aiden said, "We'll catch up the bill later." The waitress nodded and they left.

Aiden's chest burned with the need to bellow his frustrations into the sky. And if he was honest, his fears too. He was damned scared. Amaryllis was a live wire when on the job—she didn't think of consequences or anything but getting the criminal.

What risks would she take?

"Got her. Thank God for technology." Latchaw stabbed his phone screen.

Aiden's cell rang, and he snapped it up. Waiting for Amaryllis's sultry tones and hearing his twin brother's confused the hell out of him. "What?" he barked.

"Got a call from a guy who was run off the road by a big truck chasing a car on Mountainside. I'm about ten miles out. I'm going to engage."

Aiden's heart throbbed hard against his chest wall. He looked to Latchaw. "She's ten miles from Judd. He can intercept, but I can get there faster."

He took off for his truck while his brother's voice projected through his cell. He ended the call and leaped behind the wheel.

"Roshannon! You're fifteen miles away. Judd's closer!"

He glanced at the sheriff. "I can get there faster." He backed out like the hounds of hell were on his tail. Screeching out of the parking lot and tearing down the road. Amaryllis may be on the back road, but Aiden knew a cut off. It was bumpier, and he'd be lucky not to pop a tire. But that was the chance he had to take.

What the hell was the woman thinking to chase down Owens without backup? *Never does anything by the book. Her stubborn little ass deserves my whip.*

He passed the head of Mountainside, the road that twisted and turned its way around the mountain like a serpent lying under a rock. He spotted the thrown gravel and the tire tracks of Amaryllis's truck. With a shake of his head, he put boot to pedal and sped past the road. A few miles away was a cutoff known as Devil's Bend. In winter, you didn't dare risk taking that road, but occasionally they'd rescue a stranded hunter there.

Aiden took it now at breakneck speeds. Flying around corners so sharp they would cut through a man with lesser constitution. Or a man who wasn't terrified for the love of his life. If she managed not to wreck taking Mountainside at what—seventy miles per hour?—the only way to get Owens would be to face him down.

The man was cornered and he knew how to be slippery. All men in these parts were armed.

Damn. Aiden reminded himself it was Sunday but Amaryllis would still be packing heat too. The Lord said to rest, not be stupid.

He gripped the wheel tighter going into a turn that would turn most people's stomachs. His pulse hadn't pounded this hard since that day overlooking the compound he was given direct order to fire upon. He couldn't pull the trigger on that operation, but he damn well wasn't backing down from this fight. Amaryllis's life could be at stake.

For a dizzying moment, he thought of ways this could end, even seeing the monster truck pitched off a ravine in a twisted, smoking mass of metal. He shook his head hard to clear it.

"Keep your shit together, Roshannon." He grabbed his phone to dial Amaryllis and found it without signal. Taking his eyes off the road for precious seconds meant one of his tires landed in a deep crater. The truck bottomed out, and he grunted at the impact. He gunned it and braced himself as the back tire trailed through the same hole.

He didn't hesitate to slam into the gas pedal again. His chest burned way more than it should. He'd only feel this sweat-drenching fear if one of his family members was in trouble — and that must mean Amaryllis meant a whole lot more to him.

He swallowed hard around the lump in his throat. He fucking loved her. There was no "falling for her." It was a done deal—he'd taken the plunge, head first.

His phone vibrated that a bunch of missed calls were coming in now that he'd picked up service again. He didn't look away from the road because now he was really in the thick of it. Switchbacks he couldn't navigate fast enough. He had to get there, had to stop Owens before Amaryllis bit off more than she could chew alone.

When his phone rang, he stabbed a button and slapped it to his ear. "Amaryllis?"

"It's me." Judd. "I'm two miles out. If I had to guess, I'd say you're navigating Devil's Bend right now?"

"Yeah, little hard to talk. Driving this road's like being a flea on a dog's back while he shakes. But I'll still get there before you do."

"Competitive, aren't we?"

"Judd, so help me, if I could punch you right now—"

"Cool it. We need a plan. Whoever gets there first is going to blockade the road. I've called for backup, and my closest deputy is five minutes behind me. I told him to step on it and join up."

"What the hell're you guys doing in my county anyway?"

"Had a bail jumper. We were helping out Wes."

"Shit—Wes'll be crossing our paths too?"

"Looks like. He's three minutes away. Now they'll be coming in hot. How well can Amaryllis handle herself?" Judd asked.

He thought of her maneuvering that big-ass truck into the small parking spot without a blink of trouble. "Very well."

"So we don't have to worry about her not being able to stop in time and plowing into us."

He hoped to hell not, but road chases often ended in wrecks. He set his jaw. "We've got this, Judd. Can't talk now. See you when I get there."

* * * * *

Amaryllis felt high from the buzz of adrenaline running through her system. Her fingers tingled and her face felt hot. She'd had her gaze fixed on the taillights of the car in front of her for what felt like hours. She blinked away the graininess, clearing her vision.

The car swerved right and left. As if that old trick would throw her off. There couldn't be another road leading from this gravelly path to hell, and Owens wasn't going to break away.

She needed her weapon. If he made a sudden cut and run, trying to escape on foot, as most people did after being chased for a long time, she couldn't take a minute to grab her 9mm from her handbag.

She cursed her lack of preparedness, but she *had been* headed to the coin laundry, where her only threat was dryer lint and someone else's lost sock left in the corner.

Pushing a breath out through her nose, she gauged her speed. She'd hit seventy-eight a couple times on a straight stretch, and the truck had felt loose underneath her, like a single stone rolling a millimeter under her tire could send her careening off into the deep ravine. Who the hell decided this road didn't need guardrails? Fucking Wyoming.

She grinned and wasn't sure if she was losing her damn mind or just thinking of the straight-laced lawman who'd claimed her heart. Aiden *was* Wyoming to her, bigger than the state, larger than life. Every proud inch of the man excited her beyond reason and if that wasn't telling, she didn't know what was.

Without a doubt he was on her tail. She prayed he wouldn't do anything stupid to catch up to her — this road couldn't be navigated faster than she already was. And she thanked God for the big, meaty, aggressive treads on the monster truck's tires. How Owens was staying on the road had to be pure will and dumb luck. The car fishtailed so often that her heart had stopped jumping when it happened, taking it as normal.

She had to end this soon. Surely there was a way to gain enough ground to run him off the road without killing him. There was a high bank on the left with a drop to the right. In places, she couldn't see the bottom, and more often than not, the treetops were level with the truck. Again—who the hell didn't put guardrails on a road like this?

Her phone rang. Dammit, if she took the call, she might miss an opportunity to gain on Owens.

It rang several more times before she couldn't take it anymore and blindly stabbed at a button on her screen. "Long."

"I know it's you. Dammit, what the hell are you think—" Aiden's angry tone flooded her ear. She abruptly cut off the call and dropped her phone in the cup holder.

Oh, she'd pay for that one later. He would not be happy with her hanging up on him.

So she'd let him whip her a little and make him feel in control again. By this time, she knew that was how he dealt with stressful situations and gained the upper hand in life. She was good with it—more than good. Aiden was a damn fine lover, and she never wanted to leave his bed, if she was honest.

The idea of sticking around Crossroads held an appeal. But what if the county couldn't afford to keep her on? Or what if Aiden didn't want her?

She shook off that personal train of thought and racked her brain for ways to end this fucking chase. Perspiration ran in rivulets down her spine and she didn't even have a clean shirt to put on because they were all in the laundry bag.

"Think, Amaryllis." Usually chases didn't last long before the runner got too stressed and bailed. But Owens had a lot at stake. If he was heading this huge operation, and she believed he was, then he was looking at a big sentence. A lot of years behind bars. Cattle thieving was no slap on the wrist.

The taillights of Owens' car swerved far to the right. She sucked in a gasp, seeing her moment. She stomped the gas and hit the same patch of gravel that had made him lose it. Only her tires were better and she had more determination.

Gaining precious ground as he lost it skidding on gravel, she used the pit maneuver that would bring this whole chase to an end.

Using the front of her vehicle, she tapped the corner of his. Metal screeched over metal. She rocked forward at the impact. Owens's front end whipped to the side and up the bank to wrap around a thick tree trunk clinging to the mountainside.

"Crap!" She braked before she rolled over the car. She did not want to kill the man, just stop him. The car came to a stop, and she lunged for her bag. Luckily, her hand landed on her 9mm and she didn't need to upend her purse to find her weapon.

She yanked it out of her bag and threw open the door.

* * * * *

"Holy fuck." Aiden came to the intersection and didn't see any trace of the chase. No ruts in the gravel, not a breath of wind coming his way. They had to be wrecked on Mountainside.

He took the turn, gritting his teeth as gravel shifted. Damn Amaryllis. Behind him, he caught the whoop of a siren and glanced in the rearview mirror. Judd was on his tail with a deputy's cruiser and Wes's truck behind that.

Setting the example, he took off at a speed the devil himself couldn't keep up to. But Judd stayed on his tail. Ahead was a curve and warning bells went off in his head. He hit the brakes, slowing slightly as he rounded the bend.

There they were. The red monster truck on all four wheels and a silver car with the front end wrapped around a tree on the bank.

Amaryllis stood there looking like an avenging angel, legs braced apart, her weapon trained on the car window.

Time slowed as Aiden seemed to take ages to reach them. His ears were ringing, and he was sure his blood pressure was over the roof. He spun gravel with his abrupt stop and barely registered the other car doors slamming as his brother, cousin and one of Judd's deputies followed him.

All he could see was Amaryllis. She was alive, on her feet, her expression fierce.

"Get out of the car!" Her demand echoed through his bones, uniting his brain with his body again, and he launched forward to aim his weapon at the passenger window.

"Get out! Hands up!"

Amaryllis glanced over the car at him, and he felt his heart lift. He fucking loved her and no way was he losing her.

She also wasn't getting away with this. Tonight he'd turn her over his knee—right

after he kissed her senseless and held her until
the shaking inside him stopped.

Chapter Fourteen

"Damn, Amaryllis, you musta been *flying* down this road. How fast were you going? Seventy? Eighty?" Judd's question made Aiden's eyes roll back in his head, and Amaryllis knew she had to answer carefully.

"Something like that."

Aiden's hands clenched into fists at his sides.

"Great driving." Judd's comment had all the other lawmen gathered around Owens' wrecked car bobbing their heads in agreement.

"Your timing was perfect. If you'd tried that maneuver any sooner, you would have both gone over the ravine."

"That's enough." Aiden used his shoulders to barrel through the group. He grabbed Amaryllis by the forearm. "I need to talk to you."

His warm, strong fingers grounded her. When she looked into his eyes, she saw all the things he wasn't saying.

He drew her away from the wreckage and didn't stop walking until they were out of earshot. Turning to face her, eyes dark, jaw grim. "You scared the fuck outta me."

"I know, and I'm sorry for it. I was doing the only thing I knew how to do. If I'd hesitated, we would have lost Owens. He would have gone into hiding and who knows when we would have nabbed him?"

"Would it have been so bad if we didn't? If you would be staying in Wyoming longer?"

Her breath caught. "What are you saying, Aiden?"

"Dammit, woman, I'm saying I'm not ready for you to go. I don't want you to go." He grabbed her by the upper arms and yanked her close enough that his piney scent gripped her and her body stirred with the want to feel him moving inside her.

Heart pounding, she met his gaze. The steely gray of his eyes intensified by his strong emotions—anger and worry and something else. Something that sent liquid heat pooling in her core.

"I don't have to fly out tomorrow just because we think we've got the leader of the ring. There's a lot left to investigate."

"It's more than that." His gruff voice sounded with irritation, as if he was annoyed with himself for not putting his thoughts into words better. "I don't want you to go at all."

"Aiden..."

"Tell me how you feel, Amaryllis. If you don't feel what I'm feeling, I have to know now." His grip tightened until she came onto tiptoe flush to his body.

She leaned into him, searching his gaze. "I don't know what you're feeling, so how can I say?"

He worked his jaw. "I was out of my head knowing you were on this road, taking risks. Your life in jeopardy."

"I got the job done. Not a scratch on me."

"I know that! You're a capable, strong woman and I love that about you but at the same time, it drives me crazy."

She'd never seen him this way, so uncontrolled.

"If I stick around I'm bound to do something else you disapprove of. Against the rules."

"Dammit." He swooped in and kissed her soundly. His lips hard and unmoving over hers. When he drew back, she gaped at him.

"Everyone can see us."

"I don't give a damn. Let them look." He cupped her face and kissed her again, his tongue hot and urgent inside her mouth. She returned his kiss stroke for stroke until she was shaking for more.

Aiden broke free, panting. "I'm saying I care about you, Amaryllis. You make me feel things I never have."

"Like stomach cramps?" Her tease died on her lips as his gaze pierced through her.

"Exactly like stomach cramps. The kind you get when you're in love with a reckless woman."

Her lips parted on a gasp. He loved her? Aiden Roshannon had actually just told her that he loved her?

He slid the pad of his thumb down her cheek to her jaw. "Tell me what you're thinking."

"I'm thinking I don't know how I feel about being compared to stomach cramps."

"You said it first."

"But I'm thinking I love you too."

A sound in his chest, part rumble, part growl made her nipples squeeze into hard pebbles. Aiden hauled her against him again as he slammed his mouth over hers. This kiss was no tender, we-just-admitted-our-love-mingled-with-stomach-cramps kiss. He kissed her with an insistence that was almost an oath.

"You've been driving me nuts for weeks."

"I won't apologize," she whispered as he nibbled her lips.

"You will if I get you on your knees with my paddle on your bare ass."

"Nope." She ran her tongue over his lower lip, drawing another primal noise from him. "Then I'll only beg."

"Damn. Go get in my truck. I'll tell everyone we have to go talk to Owens about his nephew and they can handle clearing the vehicles here."

Dazed, she blinked up at him. He loved her and she wanted to show him how strong her feelings were. Right now.

Shirking her duties for once couldn't hurt, could it? After all, there was a capable force on the scene in the other Roshannon men.

She nodded, and he let her go with a gentle nudge. "Go to the truck."

After she'd climbed into the passenger's seat, her knees let her know that her adrenaline rush was over. In minutes, she'd gotten her criminal *and* her lover had admitted what was in his heart for her.

Watching him through the windshield, she admired everything about him. From the way his hat perched in that cocky way atop his head to the jeans hugging his carved ass. He spoke with the group for a while. Judd slapped him on the back and Wes nudged him with a shoulder. Judd's deputy threw his head back to laugh at something they said.

When Aiden started back, he met her gaze through the windshield. Need shot through her. She pressed her thighs together, her body on high alert.

She loved this man, and no way could she return to Texas and leave him.

He got into the truck and looked at her. "Latchaw's holding two other guys thought to be involved with the thefts back in Crossroads. Judd and the others are taking Owens and we'll meet them there."

Damn. So they wouldn't have their time alone.

He planted a hand on the back of her seat and twisted to back up. He turned around and started down the road where he'd come. When he rested a hand on her thigh, his eyes were warm, his touch solid. "I don't intend to take you back to the station yet."

A thrill hit her belly. "Seems like there's plenty of back roads to get lost on."

He gave a single nod, lips curling. "That's right." He walked his fingers up her thigh and nestled his hand against her crotch. Her pussy throbbed at the contact, her panties damp in an instant.

"I'm going to take you down this road a ways. Stop the truck, spread your legs and take you the way you need, doll."

"Yes…"

He took the turns faster.

"This road's even twistier than the one I drove. And you made it here plenty quick. So how fast were *you* going?" she asked.

"You tell me first."

"No way." She wasn't getting chewed out for doing her job.

"Then you'll never know."

"Let's see if this makes you talk." She unbuckled her seatbelt and moved so she could lean across the console and rest her head in his lap. With her breath fanning over his fly, his cock bulged in seconds. She worked at his belt, and he scooted down in the seat to give her better access. By the time she had his shaft free, she was burning to take him in her mouth.

And boy, was he ready. His cock head purple, shiny with precum. She snaked out her tongue and lapped it. Around and around the head until his groans became more urgent.

He suddenly slammed on the brakes and threw the truck in park. One hand on her nape, he drew her down over his cock, forcing her to take him deep. Her lips brushed the short pubic curls at the base of his length, and she inhaled his spicy clean scents.

"Fuck, you're so good at that. Suck my cock and show me what a good sub you are."

She shivered at his words. He ran his hand down to her breast, cupped it too gently for her tastes. She wanted that roughness, needed him to show her with his body how much he wanted her.

She hollowed her cheeks and sucked his length while running her tongue around his shaft.

"Damn. Stop. Get up here." He dragged her up and pulled her across the console completely to sit in his lap. She wrapped her arms around his neck.

"I want you, Aiden. Take me."

His eyelids lowered over his smoldering stare. He opened the door and got out with her balanced in his arms as he walked to the back of the truck.

One-handedly, he popped the tailgate and lowered it. With the skill of a real lover and country boy, he climbed in with her still in his arms, hardly jostling her. When he lay her on a blanket, she looked around in surprise.

"You planned this."

"Not exactly. Been carrying it around for days, hoping to get you alone on a back road."

He settled between her thighs, pushing his erection against the V of her legs.

Passion rolled through her as she held him close, her face buried against his neck. "I don't want to leave Wyoming, Aiden. What do you think Latchaw'd say to making me your permanent partner?"

He pushed back enough to look down into her eyes. Happiness made his glimmer and his rugged smile cut through his cheek like a lazy river through granite. "I'd say he'll be pretty damn happy to have one of the best rangers in the US here in Crossroads."

She smiled. Aiden was man enough not to be threatened by her strength and skill—he embraced it. After she'd figured that out, falling in love had been easy.

"Now." He stopped nibbling her neck long enough to fix her in his gaze. "You scared the hell out of me. And that means you have to do everything I say right now."

Excitement had her trembling. "I agree to those terms."

"Good. Because I want you happy. And naked." He reached for the hem of her top. His callused fingers burned over her flesh as he worked to her bra clasp. In seconds, her breasts were free and he cupped them. His cock bulged against her, and her pussy pulsated in answer.

"Unbutton your jeans."

Holding her gaze, she did his bidding.

"Zipper too."

She felt the vibration of each tooth as she eased it down.

"Bet you're hot and wet. Slide your fingers into your panties and feel your pussy for me."

Need exploded inside her. To the beat of her heart and the rumble of his voice, she sank her fingers into her panties. A gasp hit her lips. Juices coated her hand, and her clit throbbed.

"Fuck yeah. Stroke your folds for me. Tell me how good it feels."

"Oh my God." She panted as she strummed her hard pearl and down to her wet opening. "It feels so good, Aiden. I need you to touch me."

"How wet are you?"

"Drenched." Her voice came out on a rasp.

Overhead, the sun and sky only added to the experience. Being out in the open this way stimulated her until she was out of her head. She swirled her finger around her clit.

"I need you to lick me, Aiden. Eat my pussy."

"Fuck. You're so goddamn beautiful. Pull your hand free and let me taste."

She removed her hand from her panties. He caught her wrist and drew her wet fingers to his lips, inhaling and sucking them into his mouth simultaneously. She drowned in a sea of desire. Each flick of his tongue sent stabs of lust deep.

When he'd licked her clean, he let go of her hand. She curled it around his nape, drawing him down to kiss him, sharing her flavors. His growl shook her.

"I can't wait anymore, Aiden. I love you. I need you inside me."

"I love hearing you beg. Raise your hands above your head and don't move them."

As she lay on the blanket under the big Wyoming sky, Aiden stripped off his clothes. Every cut and swell of his chest seemed larger than life. Staring at him made her lick her lips. And hearing the clink of his belt buckle had her pulse racing.

He shucked clothes and boots. His hat was long gone.

"Aiden..."

"Let me look at you a minute. Lying there nude, staring up at me with those big brown eyes." His voice was gritty, the vein in his neck flickering.

For long heart beats he held her gaze. All the love welled up and a tear trickled from the corner of her eye.

"Amaryllis." He blanketed her with his body, hard to soft, scorching hot skin to skin. He kissed away her tear.

"I'm just so happy to have found you when I wasn't even looking. When I didn't know what I wanted or needed from life."

He caressed her cheek, searching her eyes. "I know. I wasn't whole after leaving the Marines and couldn't figure out what would fill that space in me. Then I saw you on that Skype call and you rocked my world."

She giggled. "Did not. You didn't like me."

"I liked you fine—when you weren't talking."

She disobeyed by moving her hand and cuffing him in the ear. He grasped her hand, fingers closing gently, and leaned in to claim her lips.

* * * * *

Each small noise erupting from Amaryllis's throat sent Aiden reeling. He'd never made love before, but with Amaryllis, there didn't seem to be anything else. Her curves threatened to undo him. Barely let him hang onto his control.

With her arms pinned overhead to the blanket and her sweet thighs cradling his hips, he sank into her.

Sweet inch by sweet inch.

Heat enveloped him all the way to his balls. He rocked into her, filling her in one deep shove.

Their shared moan was caught by the breeze trickling down from the mountains. He knew it would bring the scents of pine and woods but all he could smell was *her*.

"Spread wide for me, doll. Pull your legs up."

She obeyed and he drove another fraction deeper. Her cry resounded through his soul. He closed his eyes and let himself feel every inch as he withdrew his cock.

Plunged again. She slid on the blanket by the force. "I love your tits bouncing as I fuck you. Grab them and hold them together for me."

"Oh God," she whispered, cupping her breasts. Her nipples were deep pink, begging for his tongue. Dipping his head, he lapped one and then the other while he sank into her body.

He grazed her nipple with his teeth. Her throaty noise hit him full force. His balls clenched, and he had to still his movements for the count of ten or he'd blow.

"You're moving out of the B&B and into my place this evening."

The sexual haze on her face told him she hadn't really registered his words. But he needed her to know before he lost his mind entirely how much he wanted her with him. Sure, it had only been weeks since they'd met, and only a few days in person, but there wasn't anybody else suited to him like Amaryllis.

"I want you with me. In my bed. Tied to my bed. Bent over my bed as I spank your round little ass." He reached under her and squeezed her cheek hard enough to make her cry out.

She nodded, lips plump from being bitten. "I need you. All of you."

The fact she loved his darker side only made him slip more deeply in love with her. He ground his hips. Pleasure shot through them both. With a groan, he began to move. Faster, deeper. She spread her thighs as far as she could, and he drew her ass up into his every thrust.

"I'm going to fill you with my cum until it's running out of you."

"Yes! Aiden, I'm close. Master, can I come for you?" Her hair tumbled around her face, and he couldn't look away from her beauty.

"Wrap your arms around me."

She did, and he lifted her off the blanket, supporting her as he fucked into her so hard the truck rocked on its tires.

"Come for me. Now."

At the demand, her body clenched. Tightened. She threw her head back as a primal scream came from her. Her wet heat clamped around his cock was too much—he came in hard, fast spurts, over and over.

* * * * *

Aiden kept throwing Amaryllis dark looks throughout their process of questioning not only Billy Owens but six other men who had just been arrested in connection to the cattle rustling ring. She didn't know what Aiden could be thinking to eye her that way in front of their work colleagues, but she couldn't deny she felt a little flushed from it.

Billy Owens sat in handcuffs, looking bored as Amaryllis got up and circled the long table to him. The other suspects had spilled their guts already, but she knew there were more people involved than Billy was saying. If they didn't catch every single man or woman who'd stolen or butchered the ranchers' cattle, then the problem would arise again.

She'd seen it many times in Texas.

She leaned against the table a foot away from Billy, crossed her ankles and folded her arms as she stared at him.

He wore a bruise and cut on his forehead from their earlier activities, and she didn't feel a bit sorry for it. Too bad he hadn't busted his nose too.

"Billy. We all know you aren't telling us everything." She used her special tone—the one with a hint of disappointment hardly any momma's boy could withstand. Men were men, after all. They didn't like to disappoint.

He swung his stare to her, eyes cold. "What do you think I should tell you? You know about the old grocery store and the auctions."

"Tell me about the first cow you stole. How you led it off with a bucket of food and it went right into your trailer."

He smiled sardonically. "Sounds like you already know the story."

"I'd like to hear it from you. Whose cow was it?"

Getting a guy to talk about his crimes was like pulling teeth, unless he was proud of his activities. Often criminals enjoyed telling people what they'd done because they felt superior in intelligence to have evaded the law so long.

His lips twisted. "My uncle's."

There was a stirring behind her where Aiden, the deputies and sheriff sat.

"You saw an opportunity of earning some money so you took it."

"Wouldn't have if he'd lent me the money I need. I came to Crossroads to ask him for some cash to bail me out of a debt. In over my head with a mortgage and several loans that I'm behind in payments on. Kirby's the only family I have with more money than he needs."

She nodded. "So you feel entitled to him helping you."

"Yeah." Billy shifted as if to fold his arms, but his hands were cuffed behind the chair. "Why the hell shouldn't he lend me money? I woulda paid it back."

"You saw the money grazing in his fields and you took your chance."

"First one was easy. I took a few others and he never suspected."

"You made friends and they wanted a cut," Amaryllis prompted.

"No. That dumbass neighbor of his, Mitchell, caught me one night. I told him I'd give him a half a beef for his family or to sell if he'd keep quiet."

"Which led to Mitchell procuring more butchered cows to sell."

He nodded. "Then Mitchell told a friend who told his brother and pretty soon there were more of us out there. Some selling the live cattle, some the meat."

"Instead of you paying off the debts you'd accrued, the same debts you say brought you to Crossroads to ask your uncle for help, you went out and bought a stereo system for your truck and a Polaris sport utility vehicle."

Billy gave her a bored look. "Why ya asking if ya already know?"

"It's not a question." She straightened and flipped the chair next to Billy backward to straddle it. She stared at him, aware of Aiden's tense pose and the other lawmen seated around the table ready to spring if Billy so much as cussed at Amaryllis.

She folded her arms on the chair back and rested her chin on them. "We need names. There are at least five more men we believe worked with you."

"Why should I tell you anything?"

"Because withholding the information will only earn you more time on your sentence. Right now, you're looking at ten years minimum. Eight if you get out on good behavior, but I'll make damn sure the judge knows you weren't cooperative."

Silence filled the room. Billy stared right through her. His glare rolled right over her. The man could dick around all he wanted, but she wasn't backing down from her demands.

She raised her chin off her hands and met his stare. "Names."

"Fuck you."

Aiden was on his feet, his chair rocketing across the room, so fast that Amaryllis didn't have time to blink. Aiden rounded the table and grabbed Billy by the scruff of the neck. He bent down to glare into his eyes. In a deadly calm voice, he said, "You will show Ms. Long some respect."

Amaryllis stood and leaned toward Billy from the opposite side. With both of them breathing down his neck, Billy caved.

"Fine. I'll give you some names."

"You will give us the *right* names," Aiden commanded.

"Yeah."

When Hoyt was finished jotting down all the names Billy recited, they had a shocking list. The people involved in Crossroads weren't people they'd ever suspect. Sons of respected business owners, and even a daughter of the man who owned Delaney's diner. Amaryllis thought she might have even seen the girl waiting tables.

Sheriff Latchaw sent out warrants for their arrests, and as the deputies rolled out to track down the suspects, Aiden and Latchaw dealt with some paperwork.

That left Amaryllis to go inside Aiden's office, close the door and wait for him. Casting a look around the small space, she considered the possibilities. Since their romp in the truck, she realized she liked having a new place to seek pleasure.

Aiden's desk would serve well enough. His wheeled chair creaked, she remembered from seeing him sit in it. Other than that, a short span of wall between the door and a filing cabinet could be a good place for him to pin her.

The window presented a problem, because it overlooked the parking lot and anybody pulling in could see them.

A thrill hit her belly.

She spun his chair and sank into it. Then she unbuttoned the top three buttons of her denim shirt to reveal an ample amount of cleavage. Crossing her thighs in a seductive pose, she waited. Hoping one of the deputies didn't barge in and find her looking like the seductress. Or worse, Latchaw. The man had just given her a permanent spot on their team, and she couldn't think of a more terrible way to thank him.

The quiet in the office settled into her consciousness. Without the crime to distract her, her mind wandered. To packing up her few possessions from the B&B and taking them to Aiden's house. Of him giving her the closet and then discussing flying back to Texas with her to get the rest of her things.

It was a big step—a huge one, actually. Normally it would terrify her. Hell, just the idea of owning the small farm in Texas had left her with misgivings and butterflies, but moving in with Aiden... It felt right.

A step sounded outside the door. Her muscles tightened and her heart fluttered in anticipation.

"Thanks, Latchaw. I'll get that written up." Aiden opened the door and blinked at Amaryllis seated behind his desk.

She gave him a flick of her eyes and stretched her shoulders back, giving him a good view of her breasts. "Howdy, Special Investigator."

He closed the door quietly. "Need to get myself a lock."

"Uh-huh." She uncrossed her legs in a move like an exotic dancer, swinging her leg up and wide.

His eyelids lowered over his smoldering gray eyes. "What's going on here, hmm? Are you trying to draw me into doing something against the law, Ms. Long? I've seen you in action, and I know firsthand you're good at that. Or is this just you being reckless again? Bucking the rules."

She stood and moved around the desk to grab him by the shirtfront. Going on tiptoe, she whispered against his lips, "Or maybe I just want you to take me in your office."

"We might get caught."

"That's the exciting part."

"Damn, what have I gotten myself into with you, woman?" He growled against her lips before claiming them and lifting her at the same time. Pulling her up into his arms and crushing her mouth under his.

His kisses were dizzying, and she realized she was holding her breath. With a gasp, she filled her lungs again. He moved to the desk and set her on the corner facing the window.

"If you fuck me like this, everyone can see your bare ass through the window." She smiled at him and batted her lashes.

"Guess I'll have to take that chance."

"Why, Special Investigator Roshannon, how shocking." She plucked at his shirt buttons until the fabric hung open to reveal the line of muscled perfection.

He caught her hair in his fist and wrapped it tight to her scalp. Then, drawing her head back, he sucked on the arch of her throat. Goosebumps broke over her, and she couldn't get his pants down fast enough. In seconds, hers were puddled at her ankles and she was bent over the desk.

He poised at the root of her. Breathing hard in her ear. "I don't have time to torment you right now, but rest assured later you will be tied to my bed and introduced to my flogger."

A shiver snaked down her spine. His grip on her hair stung deliciously. "Good."

"Good, what?"

"Master," she breathed.

He entered her in one slick glide. Buried to the root. She braced her hands on the desk and pushed back to meet his every thrust.

"You like taking risks, but this is as far as you'll go now." He grunted as he pushed deep again.

She wanted to say no way would she obey that command, but she'd save the argument for the next time they were out on an investigation and she took a liberty that bagged them their criminal. For now, let Aiden think he had the upper hand outside of their sexual playground. Outside, they were on equal footing. Partners.

On his next thrust, her pussy contracted hard. Him hitting every sensitive nerve ending as he stretched her to full capacity. She stopped breathing again. Three more jerks of his hips and she came in a hard rush.

Hot spurts filled her at the same time. The desk groaned under his assault, and she wondered if anybody could hear what was going on in the small office.

Then he bit into the side of her neck and squeezed her nipple at the same time, making her forget anything but him.

Aiden, her lawman. There was something about a man who strutted around packing a .40, looking hot as hell, but could also fuck her this thoroughly—and make her heart fuller than she ever would have dreamed.

"Fuck, woman, you're gonna kill me." He collapsed against her back, strumming her hard nipple with his thumb.

She wiggled until he disconnected from her body and turned into his arms. "I promise to keep you on your toes, Roshannon."

He clapped a hand on her ass, a light swat that promised so much more. "I look forward to… Every. Damn. Moment." He kissed her softly, a swirling of their tongues that spoke of the emotions that would meld them together for the rest of their lives.

THE END

****SPECIAL BONUS SCENES****

A note from Em Petrova:

Sometimes in the writing process, an author finds the book isn't working. When I began writing *Something About a Lawman*, my idea was to flash back to the Roshannon boys as youths and give the readers an insight into how they all became involved with the law.

Toward the end of the book, I realized these scenes were bogging me down, and I cut them. But an author never deletes her precious words! Besides, I thought you would like reading them. Please enjoy the cut scenes from *Something About a Lawman*.

Twenty years ago

"You wouldn't know what a real set of balls looked like even if you saw 'em, Wes."

Wes made a scoffing noise. "Neither would your momma."

"You take that back!" Judd fisted his hands, his gray eyes shooting the hell-fire only an eight-year-old boy could when his cousin spoke badly about his momma.

Aiden looked on at his twin and cousin about to throw down over a momma joke. Technically, the insult was aimed at their father too, because surely their mother would have seen *his* real set of balls. But Aiden wasn't about to bring it up. They were acting so stupid and babyish.

"What ya gonna do? Your momma hasn't seen any real balls because your daddy doesn't have any!" Wes danced around, waving his skinny arms.

Judd raised his fists and took a swing, his noodle arm seeming to wobble in the Wyoming breeze.

They were all skinny country boys. They biked for miles to hunt and fish and worked their hides off on their family ranch. But their cousin Wes was shorter than they were and as skinny as a stalk of corn. More than once Aiden and his twin Judd had to pull bullies off him before he got pounded into the dirt.

Judd shoved Wes, and he lowered his head to ram him like a bull—his only defense was his big, hard head.

Aiden turned his back on the pair and started picking his way along the bank of the stream. He had a full stringer of trout for their dinner, and he wanted to hurry home so his momma could start putting them into the hot oil. His stomach was turning inside out and they had a long walk home.

"Aiden!" Judd's call made him throw a look over his shoulder. His twin was holding his own with Wes. They were both still on their feet and nobody was bleeding. He didn't need any help. He faced forward again. "Hey, dummy! Aren't you gonna defend your own mother?"

"Momma jokes are too stupid to bother over. C'mon, Judd. Don't you want supper?"

A second later he heard footsteps behind him, and then his brother was next to him. Wes flanked his other side and they started toward home. Nobody talked for a full minute.

"Think your momma would care if I have supper with you?" Wes asked.

"If I tell her what you said about her, she will." Judd thrust his jaw forward.

"Quit bickering. Sick of listening to it. A man needs some damn peace once in a while," Aiden said.

The boys sucked in gasps of shock.

Judd's eyes were round. "You swore."

"You sounded just like your old man," Wes added in awe.

Aiden's mouth twisted in a smile. "Let's just get home. I'm hungry and these fish are heavy."

They followed the stream, meandering back through the valley. The mountains were jagged spikes against the deep blue sky, and the air was clearer here than in any other part of Wyoming. Aiden would know—he'd been to all twenty-three counties. When his pa went to cattle auctions, they drove all over the state. Aiden loved those times, standing next to his father while they inspected cattle. His pa had even let him place a bid or two in the past. When he grew up, he wanted to take over the ranch.

Wes squatted to look at a fat toad next to the water's edge. Before he could get his hands around it, the toad leaped. Wes lunged. Aiden and Judd laughed as he tumbled down the bank into the water. He scrambled to his feet, dripping and his face screwed up with anger.

"You guys—" He cut off, his voice strangled.

Aiden looked at him more closely.

"Did he swallow a bug or something?" Judd asked.

"No, something's actually wrong." Aiden rushed down the bank and thrashed his way into the stream. Water rushed into his boots, filling them up to his shins. "You okay, Wes?"

He pointed. Aiden followed his finger to an overhanging branch and a foot visible just beneath. Not just a foot. A foot attached to a body, attached to a torso. And when Aiden moved to the side, he spotted the face of a man, bloated, staring.

"What the hell?" Judd drew up beside them and stared at the dead man. He folded at the waist and puked into the stream.

"He's been dead a while," Wes managed, sounding as if his stomach hung out in his throat too.

Aiden nodded. He'd seen people dead before. An old neighbor lady who'd made delicious batches of peanut butter cookies and their grandma Caroline. But those people had been cleaned up, eyes shut so they appeared to be sleeping.

The bile rose in the back of Aiden's throat too, but he gulped it down.

"What do we do?" Wes pushed his heavy brown hair from his eyes.

"I think we should run to the road and flag down a car and tell somebody." Judd was as pale as the underbelly of a fish.

Aiden held up a hand. "I'm oldest here—"

"By four minutes!" Judd retorted.

"And by five months," Wes added.

"Still oldest. So I'm taking charge." He looked at the man again. Could they manage to drag him? He'd be heavy. He was wet.

Maybe Judd's idea was best.

"Town's closer than home, if we run straight through the woods. We go now, we'll get there in an hour tops and we can tell the sheriff."

The boys looked at him. "What about the fish?" Judd asked.

"And that big dinner?" Wes didn't look like he was going to barf anymore.

"The fish should keep. Maybe we can buy some ice and put them in a bag when we get to town. C'mon." He gave the body one last appraising look and headed up the bank. He paused to dump out his boots and then set off again without a backward look. His brother and cousin followed, and Aiden didn't tell them his knees were shaking.

Twenty years ago

Wes released a long, low whistle as they approached the sheriff's office. For the last mile of walking, all Judd and Wes had talked about was supper. Judd's stomach had been growling so loud that Aiden thought about starting a fire and roasting a fish or two over it on a stick. But they'd pushed on, and here they were, about to talk to one of the most intimidating men on the planet.

Sheriff Rawlins. Six-foot-four with a chest the size of a bull. He was rumored to take down everything from petty thieves to cattle rustlers to murderers with only a glare. One look from that steely-eyed stare and a man confessed, it was told up and down these parts.

"You go first," Wes said. "You're oldest."

"You never think me being oldest gives me an advantage any other time."

Judd elbowed him. "Go on. You walk up to the door first."

Aiden looked at the door. Painted white, like the rest of the building. Didn't look so scary if he thought about it being a place of business, like a bait shop.

He steeled his jaw and walked up to the door. His brother and cousin were at his heels, crowding close. Aiden shrugged. "Give a man some room, would ya?"

Wes stepped back but Judd didn't budge. Aiden figured his twin was experiencing that connection, same as he was. Each of them swore when one was scared, their heart beat double. It made him woozy, but he didn't have time for that crap right now.

He opened the door and stepped inside with Judd plastered to his back. Wes tripped over the threshold and nearly fell on his face.

From behind a desk, a woman looked up at them.

Aiden swallowed.

"Can I help you boys?"

"Uhh." They hadn't figured anybody besides the sheriff would be here, so being met by a kindly smile made Aiden want to weep with relief. He wouldn't, though. He firmed his jaw again.

"We need to talk to the sheriff."

She got up and came around her desk to smile at them wider. "He's out on a call right now, but I can take a message."

"It's the sheriff we need to see," Wes spoke up.

Judd threw him a shut-up-idiot look. Aiden had to admit, talking to this nice woman instead of the beast of a sheriff was looking better by the second.

"Everyone needs to see the sheriff, son. But sometimes people have to tell me what they need to speak with him about and then I pass on the message."

Aiden nodded and then stopped. He glanced over the woman. She was older, with gray in her hair, looking a little frail in a baggy pair of pants and a sweater. How in heck was she wearing a sweater? It was eighty degrees out. Yeah, she was definitely old. Could her heart handle what they were about to tell her?

"We'll wait," Aiden said stubbornly. He wasn't about to be responsible for her death.

Behind him, Judd's breath washed out. "You sure, brother?"

Aiden nodded.

"Well, if you're set on waiting, there's a bench outside. Could be a while."

Was mighty hot too. The fish were starting to stink.

Aiden pulled at his hat brim the way he'd seen his dad do a million times. "Thank ya, ma'am."

She smiled again and went back to her desk while the boys headed out. Aiden plunked onto the bench first and the others crammed next to him.

"What's wrong with you, thick-head?" Judd smacked the heel of his hand off Aiden's skull, knocking his hat sideways. "We coulda told that nice lady what we saw and been on our way home. I'm starving and those fish are rottin'."

Aiden looked down at the stringer of fish dangling down his thigh. He couldn't argue. But he couldn't voice his reasons for wanting to wait for the sheriff. "We'll wait," he said firmly.

Judd sighed and Wes fell silent, kicking at a pebble under the bench with the toe of his boot. What felt like hours passed. From inside, the sheriff's secretary started to hum, the sound projecting through the window like an invitation to tell her. Easy to walk back in and spill the story and be home for a late supper. Too much later and they'd miss chores, which would end in nothing till breakfast.

"What if he's gone till mornin'?" Wes asked.

Aiden looked at his cousin. He was so scrawny he probably wouldn't last till morning. Aiden swung his gaze to his twin. He was red-cheeked from the heat but wasn't sweating anymore. Probably getting heatstroke. He'd seen a cowpoke get it once and he had to be taken to the hospital.

He had to make a decision. Scare the bejeezus out of the secretary with their story or risk his family.

Family came first.

He pushed to a stand. Before he could take a step, a big old white SUV pulled up right in front of the office. Aiden didn't need to look to know the word SHERIFF was painted on the side. Everyone knew this vehicle.

"Oh shit," Judd whispered.

Aiden put out a hand. "I'll take care of it."

The sheriff climbed out and started toward the office, shoving a small notebook into his breast pocket. He stopped short when he saw the boys. "Your pa inside waitin' to talk to me?" he asked.

Aiden shook his head. "We need to talk to you about something we saw, sir."

The sheriff towered over them, his gaze as cold as the body that lay by the stream when he looked them over. "You look hot. Hungry too. I was fancyin' a chocolate cone from Amy's down the street. Seems like you could use one too."

Wes's head practically bounced off with the force of his nod and Judd's stomach rumbled in answer.

Aiden answered for them. "That would sure sit well, Sheriff."

Hours later, after a round of ice cream cones and the story about the body they'd discovered and their ideas about how it had come to be there, the sheriff drove them home. As he dropped them off at the ranch, he gave them all a smile—the first they'd ever seen on his face.

Twenty years ago

"'You leave this to me, boys. I'll take care of it.' That's what the sheriff said." Wes's face was lit by the greenish glow of the flashlight they took into the closet they used as a clubhouse. The light sat on its end, the beam spreading a dim glimmer on each of them, sitting cross-legged on the closet floor.

"Well, he's not doing his job. There's nothing in the newspaper about the murder at all." Judd picked at the frayed lace of his boot.

"You're gonna catch hell for having your boots on in the house," Aiden said.

Judd made a face. "You called an emergency meeting right after chores and there wasn't time to take them off."

"I managed to take mine off."

Wes cleared his throat pointedly. More and more their cousin was stepping up in this investigation, drawing things to order. After the three of them had spoken with the sheriff about the body they'd seen, they'd made it their mission to look after the case. When they heard nothing except that the man was dead, they'd decided to launch their own investigation.

"You're right, Wes. We have to stay on track."

"But I've got homework," Judd whined.

"We all do, dummy. Old Mrs. White gave us all the same math pages, remember?" Aiden didn't know why he was having a go at his twin. Maybe he was hungry and it smelled in this closet like stinky feet and manure off Judd's boots.

"Get on with it, guys," Wes said. "Aiden, read what you have written in your notebook this week."

He pulled out the notebook he'd bought with some spare change at the drugstore in town and proudly opened it to the second page. The words were scribbled, barely legible in the crappy light coming from the flashlight. He lowered the book and stared between Judd and Wes.

"Why we gotta meet in Wes's closet? Why can't we just sit in his room?"

"Because nobody can listen in here," Wes said. He tapped a finger on the book. "Now read."

Aiden and Judd exchanged a glance at their cousin's sudden force of character. Maybe he could start beating up his own bullies from now on.

Or maybe not. Wes was still as big as a Junebug.

Aiden read, "Nothing in newspaper. Boot tracks down at the stream near where the body was found."

Judd leaned forward, his face animated. "That's our best lead yet."

"Could be any old fisherman down there catching some trout, Judd." Aiden wasn't committed to the detail being that important.

"Or the killer could be coming back to make sure he didn't leave anything behind."

"Well, he left a boot track." Wes stretched out, kicking over the flashlight. Darkness closed around them, and Aiden wasn't feeling so good about being in the closet anymore.

"That old track didn't show us anything but somebody likes to fish the stream. I'm gonna wash up for dinner." He fumbled in the dark for the door handle, but Judd grabbed his arm as Wes righted the flashlight.

"Dude, we gotta write everything down in the murder book. That's how it's done," Judd said.

"That's right. We nail the timeline." Wes started ticking things off on his fingers. "Follow every single lead. And we keep looking at every clue even when the case goes cold."

"Guys, I think it *is* cold. If the sheriff hasn't found a suspect yet, how can we?" Aiden asked.

Judd gave him a long, solemn look like he was disappointed to have shared a womb with him. "That's why we have to keep searching. No stone is left unturned."

"That's it!" Wes said. "Tomorrow we start looking for stones."

They both stared at him.

"The stones from the creek will be muddier than anywhere else. And it's not just any mud—it's that thick brown stuff that gets all over everything."

"That's true," Judd said. "Momma yells at us all the time for dragging in creek mud."

"Yeah, and it's sticky too. It picks things up. Like pebbles." Wes opened his gray eyes wide as if they'd catch his meaning. They didn't.

"Say it plain," Aiden said.

"If the murderer went back to the creek to see if he left anything behind, the mud would stick to his boots and pick up anything he walked over, like pebbles or twigs. Then when the mud dried, those things might have fallen off."

"So if we find some rocks or sticks from the man's boots, then we could follow the trail to the murderer," Judd said excitedly.

Aiden took out his pen and wrote that all down. Then he snapped the book shut. "I'm starvin'. Let's get washed up before Momma calls us to dinner."

Twenty Years Ago

"That's it. It's all over." Aiden sat back, looking at his twin and cousin. The newspaper lay on the closet floor, the headline that the body found at the creek had been a result of natural causes. No foul play involved.

After all the discoveries the boys had made. The hours beating the path, talking to suspects and finding what they believed were leads in the case, the man had simply died of a heart attack while hiking. He'd fallen down the bank and into the water, where he'd turned his blank eyes up to God.

"Son of a bitch." Judd kicked at the notebooks scattered on the floor.

"Doesn't mean anything, guys," Wes said.

Aiden stared at him. The crack in the door afforded enough light that they didn't need the flashlight. "What are you talking about, Wes? It means he died of a heart attack, and we wasted all this time trying to hunt down a murderer."

"Yeah, but we learned a lot. At least I did. I... I think I want to do this when I grow up, guys. Go into the law. Maybe become a sheriff."

Judd and Aiden gaped at him as the realization sank in. They *had* learned a lot in the past few weeks they'd been trying to solve the crime. And they'd enjoyed doing it.

"Maybe I want to be a lawman too," Aiden said.

"Me too. I can't see myself being happy with just ranchin' the way pa does." Judd reached for the notebooks and started stacking them again.

Wes grinned at them both. "Then we keep our detective club?"

"Sure, we'll just find other crimes to solve," Judd said with excitement.

"I heard someone broke into Mrs. Craft's barn the other day and stole a bunch of stuff."

"What can Mrs. Craft even own that's worth anything?" Judd scoffed.

"Doesn't matter. Stuff was stolen, and that's a crime." Aiden lifted a brow as he looked at his brother and cousin. "What do you say? Are we takin' the case?"

Wes nodded at once and Judd followed.

"Good. Gimme a new notebook. I'll write down what I know."

Eighteen years ago

The boys were getting too large for Wes's closet. They were all twelve now, shooting up like bad weeds, Aiden and Judd's pa said. Wes was still shorter than them. Skinnier too. But he had a gangly look like a colt did right before they came into their full growth.

"So Old Thatch got his John Deere stolen yesterday. You might have heard him talkin' to Pa," Aiden said as way of opening the meeting of their detective club.

"Who can just drive off with a John Deere? Where was the key?" Wes asked.

"In the ignition," Judd said, flicking his shoelace like a tiny lasso.

Wes stretched out his long legs and kicked over the flashlight serving as light. The closet went black.

"Set that up again. I can't see my book," Aiden said.

329

"Screw that book, Aiden. It can't tell us anything we couldn't have overheard from Old Thatch talkin' to Pa." Judd still reached for the light and set it on its end so the beam spread over them like an umbrella.

Ignoring his brother's outburst, Aiden read his notes. "He went to bed at nine-thirty."

"Not unusual for a rancher," Wes added.

"Nope. And he got up once to use the bathroom. That was around three in the morning."

"God's sake, Aiden, who gives a crap when the guy took a whizz?"

He gave Judd a long look but said nothing.

"Fine. Get on with it." Judd tied his lace into a mini noose and Aiden knew who that was for.

"When he went out to the barn at six, the John Deere was missing. That means someone came between three and six."

Judd sat back, propped on his palms. "Dang, you're an Einstein, aren't ya? You can tell time."

"You know, that's it." Aiden dropped his book and lunged for his brother. He got him on the floor, legs pinned, and dug his arm across his neck.

"That's enough," Wes said. "You can't kill your twin, Aiden."

330

"Why not?" He grunted with the exertion of holding down a boy who equaled him in strength.

"You'd have to live with half a soul, that's why. You know what your twin link is like. Let him up."

Aiden looked down at his brother's sweaty face.

"If you do, I'm going to strangle you," Judd vowed.

"Can't let him up now."

"This is ridiculous. There's no room in this closet for us, let alone a brawl." Wes gathered his feet under him to stand.

"Where ya goin'?" Aiden let off his brother enough that Judd got a punch in. Head rocking, ear ringing from the blow, Aiden rolled off.

"I'm hungry, and this is a waste of time," Wes said.

Aiden stared up at him. "How are we gonna find the guy who stole the tractor? What if he steals *our* tractor? How will we do the chores around here?"

Wes stopped with his hand on the doorknob. Judd scooted into a sitting position, breathing hard with anger at being pinned down. Aiden would have to watch his back for a few hours until his twin got over his grudge.

"We have to try, guys. The sheriff is too busy hauling in people running drugs and drunk drivin' to spend time on Old Thatch's tractor. We have to help."

"Fine," Judd said.

Wes sat again, Indian-style. "Who do we know that stays up all night. Someone who can't sleep?"

The boys were silent as they thought.

"And," Aiden said slowly, "who was down at the feed store the other day asking about ways to keep grass from growing so fast because his tractor's busted?"

Judd straightened with excitement. "Mayburn," he and Wes said at the same time.

Aiden nodded. Adam Mayburn was half a tick off the bubble, his brain fried by something that had happened at his birth. He was slow, low-functioning and often prowled town at night because he couldn't sleep. Once he'd even come over to Eagle Crest and knocked on the door to ask for a drink of water. Their mom had gotten up and given him the glass of water and a cinnamon bun before sending him on his way.

Mayburn was at least forty-five years old and lived with his aging parents. They had no knowledge of half the stuff the man did.

"You know what we need to do. Go up to Mayburn's place and see if the John Deere's parked there," Aiden said.

"You think he'd just park it out in the open?" Judd asked.

"'Course he would," Wes said. "His mind doesn't work like ours. So when we going over?"

"Right now." Aiden got up and stuffed the book into the back pocket of his jeans.

"But I'm hungry," Wes said.

"You're always hungry. Your stomach has to wait. Let's go."

The Mayburns was a ten-minute walk through the fields — the freshly mown fields.

"Looks like they're ready for tillin' the earth and plantin'," Wes said, swishing his boots through the grass.

When they crested the rise and saw the Mayburns' ranch home, the gleaming green and yellow John Deere tractor parked next to it, they all stopped.

Wes fist-punched the air with a "Yaw!"

Aiden and Judd gave high-fives.

"We finally solved a case. Now let's get home and call the sheriff up and tell him. And get somethin' to eat," Wes said.

Fifteen years ago

"Hey, Aiden—" Judd broke off as he walked into Wes's room and saw Aiden sitting there beside Sadie Townsend. She sat cross-legged but her skirt barely stretched between her knees, and anybody who sat opposite her would get a glimpse of tanned thighs, and if she moved the right way, a hint of cotton panties.

"What the hell's she doing here?" Judd asked.

"Whattaya think, dumbass? She's here for the meeting." Aiden directed his gaze back to his girlfriend. She had long honey-colored hair and big blue eyes and a smile that melted every one of the boys in the ninth grade.

Sadie blushed as she looked up at Judd, and Aiden didn't know if he liked that. Maybe it'd been a bad idea to bring a girl here for their weekly detective meeting. Of course, they hadn't solved any cases in ages, and half the time they ended up just sitting around Wes's room—they'd long outgrown the closet—playing games or talking sports.

"Where's Wes?" Aiden asked, moving his body to block Sadie from Judd's view. Especially those thighs.

Judd eyed him but thankfully didn't ask why he was lying in a twisted pretzel pose in front of the girl. "He's finishing up chores Mom asked him to do for her."

"Is Wes really your brother?" Sadie asked.

Aiden and Judd stared at each other and then laughed. "Nah, where'd you hear that?"

She leaned back, her weight on her palms. "Everybody talks about it in school. That Wes doesn't have his parents because yours ran them off. Rumor is his mother really played around with your daddy and Wes is your brother."

"That's ridiculous. Wes is just a few months younger than we are."

Sadie shrugged. "Just what they say."

When Wes barged into the room, he skidded to a stop. His hat was askew, his shirt hung open with sweat standing out on his chest.

Sadie's gaze latched onto it like a hungry teen looked at a buffet. Aiden shot to his feet, blocking Wes from her view.

Judd squinted his eyes at him and then a grin broke over his face. Great—his damn twin knew what Aiden was doing.

He glared at Judd, who just smiled wider.

Sadie leaned to the side to see around Aiden's legs. She didn't even try to hide the fact she was batting her eyelashes. Obviously, she'd come with him to flirt with his brother and Wes.

"All right, meetin's over," he grumbled and stomped to the door.

Wes and Judd gaped at him. "We didn't even go over the crimes."

"Doesn't matter—we won't solve 'em anyway. C'mon, Sadie. I'll walk you home."

She got to her feet. As she passed Judd, she smiled. She threw Wes a wink. By this time, Aiden wasn't even sure he wanted to walk her home, but he had to make sure she got there safely.

When he returned, Wes and Judd were doing target practice out back. He watched them take their shots. Then he grabbed a pistol and neatly tipped shells into the chamber. He stepped up, took aim and hit the bullseye.

"You're gettin' good at that, Aiden," Judd said.

"I was picturing your face," he said coldly.

Judd stepped up to him. "Your girlfriend was flirting with *me*."

"But you were pretty damn cheerful about it." He squeezed off three more shots and turned to Wes. "That was your face." He set down the pistol and started walking away.

"New club rule, Aiden. No girls," Judd called.

"Yeah, they got no business interfering in our group and causing hard feelings." Wes put in.

Without turning around, Aiden raised a hand in agreement. He was ticked off at his brother and cousin—but mostly he was irritated with Sadie. She wasn't what she seemed, and that cut deep.

Twelve years ago

Aiden's bullet gave a low, dull *thwap* as it struck the target stuck on the hay bale three hundred yards away. He shoved another bullet in the chamber, aimed and pulled the trigger again.

"Same place," Judd said from beside him. "Don't know how you do it, bro. We've all practiced as long as you and you still shoot better."

Aiden grunted. "Thinkin' of joining the Marines."

Judd went completely still. Aiden swung his gaze to his twin, feeling a weird fluttery feeling that normally only happened when Judd was in trouble. He looked at his brother hard. Was it possible that they were connected by strong emotions too?

Judd's face mottled and his throat worked. "You're gonna leave Eagle Crest and join up?"

"Said I was thinkin' about it. Haven't signed anything yet."

"Signed anything with who? Have you talked to a recruiter?"

Aiden nodded.

"The one at school?"

He nodded again.

"I thought you were in the guidance office to switch into that study hall."

"Didn't want to tell you till I knew for sure."

"Is that why you're telling me now? Your mind's made up?"

When Judd put it that way, Aiden thought it might be.

Judd stared at him. "You talk to Momma and Pa yet?"

"No. Thought you should know first."

"So Wes doesn't know either."

"Wes doesn't know what?" Wes threw himself down in the grass next to them, sweaty from chores and smelling faintly of manure.

Aiden waited for Judd to blurt it out, but he held his tongue. Leaving Aiden to break it to his cousin—who was almost a brother—that he was breaking up the crew. They'd long ago left behind the detective club to hunt down pretty girls, but somehow leaving felt like a betrayal.

He looked to Wes. "I'm joining the Marines." He stuck another round into the rifle and nailed the third bullseye, the group of holes touching.

Wes went still. Then he picked up another bullet and handed it to Aiden. "You've got the shootin' skills. Don't know if you can take orders that well, though."

"What's that supposed to mean?" Aiden lowered his rifle.

"You just like being in charge is all. Maybe you'll be promoted fast and then you can boss everyone else around."

Aiden grunted. His nerves were jittering like popcorn in hot oil. His choice was made, he would leave Eagle Crest for something bigger than himself.

"Whatever you do, I'm behind you, bro." Wes held out a hand and Aiden took it. Squeezing as he looked into his eyes, so much like his own.

"Thank you."

"I'm going to the police academy," Judd said out of the blue.

Both looked at him in stunned surprise. "You never mentioned it."

"You didn't mention the Marines either." Judd jutted out his jaw in that stubborn way of his.

"You'll be great at it," Aiden said thickly, oddly emotional.

They both turned to Wes. "I'm not going anywhere. Staying right here. But I might take a course on firearms, maybe get licensed for a concealed carry. And I'll help your pa while you both are gone."

They nodded in unison. "That's best," Aiden said.

The club was officially dissolved, its members gone their separate ways. Who knew if they'd ever come together again the way they once had been.

**Thank you for reading SOMETHING ABOUT A LAWMAN. If you're enjoyed this book, please leave a review! Reviews make authors happy, and happy authors mean more hot books!

Em Petrova

Em Petrova was raised by hippies in the wilds of Pennsylvania but told her parents at the age of four she wanted to be a gypsy when she grew up. She has a soft spot for babies, puppies and 90s Grunge music and believes in Bigfoot and aliens. She started writing at the age of twelve and prides herself on making her characters larger than life and her sex scenes hotter than hot.

She burst into the world of publishing in 2010 after having five beautiful bambinos and figuring they were old enough to get their own snacks while she pounds away at the keys. In her not-so-spare time, she is fur-mommy to a Labradoodle named Daisy Hasselhoff and works as editor with USA Today and New York Times bestselling authors.

Find Em Petrova at:
http://empetrova.com

Other Indie Titles by Em Petrova

SOMETHIN' DIRTY

Rope 'n Ride Series
BUCK
RYDER
RIDGE
WEST
LANE

Rope 'n Ride On Series
JINGLE BOOTS
DOUBLE DIPPIN'
LICKS AND PROMISES
A COWBOY FOR CHRISTMAS
LIPSTICK 'N LEAD

The Dalton Boys
COWBOY CRAZY Hank's story
COWBOY BARGAIN Cash's story
COWBOY CRUSHIN' Witt's story
COWBOY SECRET Beck's story
COWBOY RUSH Kade's Story

Single Titles and Boxes
STRANDED AND STRADDLED

LASSO MY HEART
SINFUL HEARTS
BLOWN DOWN
FALLEN
FEVERED HEARTS
DIRTY HAIR PULLER

Firehouse 5 Series
ONE FIERY NIGHT
CONTROLLED BURN
SMOLDERING HEARTS

The Quick and the Hot Series
DALLAS NIGHTS
SLICK RIDER
SPURRED ON

Also, look for traditionally published works on her website.

Printed in the USA
CPSIA information can be obtained
at www.ICGtesting.com
LVHW051039250624
783952LV00007B/84

9 781977 932822